Bayou (

& OTHER S

Bayou Coeur

& OTHER STORIES

Larry Gray

CLEMSON UNIVERSITY PRESS

Published by Clemson University Press in Clemson, South Carolina

Editorial Assistants: Karen Stewart and Charis Chapman

Photography introduced on the cover and on frontispiece courtesy of Denise Tullier Holly

To order copies, please visit the Clemson University Press website: www.clemson.edu/press

Contents

Acknowledgments

Thanks to the staff of Clemson University Press who have shepherded my stories through the process of publication. Also thanks to Johnny Chauvin for my headshot and thanks to Denise Tullier Holly for her help in photographs for the cover design. Most of all thanks to my wife, Beth, who has given me the very best of both material and spiritual help as I went through the lonely task of putting words down on paper.

❦

Dedication

To my wife Beth who read these stories first. You are the love of my life and my partner in all that I do.

Bayou Coeur

The land around Bayou Coeur is flat. The earth barely rises above the level of the water. Look out in any direction and you can see both the curve of the earth on the distant horizon and the blue and tan surface of the water in progressive strands bisecting the land straddling all the water lines. All it takes is a breeze and water laps up on the long highway and wets the white line that runs straight as a ruler toward the Gulf.

Beside the highway there are cane fields. In the summer the cane is green and taller than any man. In the winter the fields are stripped, brown and beige and full of mud and then they're set aflame and the air is filled with the sweet and pungent smoke, and the sides of the road are littered with crushed stalks of cane and road kill. Armadillos. Snakes. Assorted dogs run down by the big cane trucks on their way to the mill.

Two miles from the closest town out beyond the fields near a skinny tree line there is a structure everyone calls Antoine's shack after the man who built it sometime after the Civil War. The shack has been home to a succession of families, none of whom have actually owned the place. No one knows who it rightly belongs to. The owner of the land is a wealthy man who lives in a big old house in Lafayette. He has grown rich from oil money and the boom of the seventies, full of enough loot to weather the bust and the uncertainties of sugar farming. He spends his days with his grandchildren and going to the races at Evangeline Downs where the loud speaker at the start of the races calls out in French, "*Ils sont parti!*" and his cronies, all wearing fedoras and baseball caps and ten gallon hats, smoke Picayune cigarettes and place their ten dollar bets.

Antoine's shack is now abandoned. The last family moved out ten years ago, no longer content to do without electricity and indoor plumbing. The wood is cypress and if it once was painted, no trace of the paint remains. It is gray and worn and stands mute and open right in the middle of the field. No one has thought to tear it down. Maybe it will stand forever. Inside there is still an iron bedstead, but no mattress. There are a few iron pots and in the yard the rusting remains of a bicycle and an old washing machine complete with a mangle. Where the outhouse once stood there is now honeysuckle and blackberry bushes and one climbing rose with thorns the length of pencil stubs.

Here and there on the interior walls there are still small strips of wallpaper, a design once popular and available at Sears and Roebuck, a tidy floral print inside stately gold and green stripes. A pile of newspapers are matted and turned to mold. There is a picture of the Immaculate Heart of Mary and a horseshoe over the lintel of the front door.

There are four kinds of houses hereabouts. Some old still rich folks live in what Yankees probably would call plantation houses. These people own the land. There are also a few newer houses, tastefully built along the old model and painted in bright bold colors. Some of these have swimming pools and barbeque pits and tennis courts. There are horses in pastures and a few heifers that will be turned into meat for the freezer. Then a few here and there houses of old fashioned ugliness, ranch style brick and built on slabs and so forever flooding, owned by the not quite wealthy who are by now used to making not quite the right decisions in life. And then there are shacks, the kind of shacks that visitors consider a scandal. "Here in America?" they ask. "People can't live like that." And these are all occupied by the workers, all black, all full of children in underpants and diapers playing in the muddy or dusty front yard, a sometime papa who they hope uses his gun only for hunting and a woman full of starch and resolve and not very good ideas, inevitably overweight with her starchy diet and an awful lot of dogs of indeterminate breed.

Surprisingly there is culture here. Folks play music. Everyone knows at least a little French. Some speak it all the time. The honky tonks and the public square and the concert hall are hosts to local chanky-chank music and to Cajun waltzes and to blues and zydeco. There are several restaurants in town that attract visitors from all over who leave their calling cards stapled to the wall and not a few rich and famous have left their pictures and their autographs after eating the local cuisine.

There is in town now a kind of quiet resignation. They had been an independent and isolated and mostly poor place that thought little or not at all about the rest of the world and then the oil boom brought people and banks and business and a whole roll call of rough necks working off shore and spending their time and money in the town. Some were college kids doing two weeks on, one week off with plans and careers and caring families. But most came from hither and yon with no more sense in their heads than a stone has kidneys. They'd work two weeks, get paid in cash, come off the boat or helicopter with a roll in their pocket—then drink and eat and whore and gamble all week and go back on Monday to the rig dead broke and satisfied, not a thought in their brain about tomorrow.

And then the oil business busted and the big companies moved to Texas and the banks closed and the little companies that depended on the big companies closed and just enough of the roughnecks got left behind to turn the town ugly and mean without the saving grace of either money or memory or family nearby.

The last family to live in Antoine's shack was one of those, a roughneck from Texas who married a local. It was the only white family ever to live in Antoine's shack and they were only there three years, just enough time to have two babies, two gunshot wounds, about a dozen breakups and beatings and finally one good divorce. He rode out of town in a pickup spitting smoke going God knows where and soon after that she was gone too leaving a lot of debt behind her but no one sad to see her go. And since then Antoine's shack has been empty.

Back in the seventies when the town was rough but prosperous one of the oil companies sent a young geologist from Ohio down there to work. He was fresh out of school, lucky in his lottery number and so he had not seen Vietnam, and unmarried. He thought this assignment would be like his Vietnam and he was not far from wrong.

On the outside he went completely native. He knew a little French and he learned more. He frequented the bars and honky tonks and he fell in love with the local music and food not to mention a couple different Cajun beauties. But on the inside he always felt foreign and removed. He'd match the roughnecks beer for beer and dance for dance but somehow at the end of the evening he'd still have money in his jeans and they'd all be tapped. Of course, he would leave sometimes between midnight and maybe on a good night two in the morning and they'd still be going strong. And he wouldn't throw around outrageous tips or visit the vans and pickups in the parking lot with the local girls or place ridiculous bets on the games on TV or the bourré games in the back room. And more often than not he'd sleep in his own bed at night and not wake up with a stranger beside him or his wallet empty on the floor under the bed.

And, of course, he had plans. Or at least dreams. Or at the very least certain expectations out of life and the roughnecks had no such thing.

He went fishing and hunting. He did a lot of things once. He skinned an alligator. He shot a wild hog. He had a narrow brush with a water moccasin. He even spent one god-awful night in jail. But he never missed a day of work and he managed to save some money and when the time felt right he left the town and went back to school in Chicago and got his Ph.D. in geology and set about an academic career with a new wife by his side he met in grad school and he moved to New Mexico where he traded in his French for Spanish and his seafood for chili and tamales and the flat water soaked prairies for the mountains. He liked the academic life and he wasn't much for looking back but an opportunity presented itself toward the end of the eighties to take a trip east and the road was not so far away and he decided to look in on Bayou Coeur and see how things had changed. That person was me.

On the parish road going into town there used to be an abundance of corrugated metal buildings full of little businesses that supplied the oil industry. The buildings were still there but almost all of them were closed. A few boasted new ownership or whole new enterprises. Most were left to rot just as the owners had left them.

In the town the main drag was pretty much empty. There was a new Dollar Store that hadn't been there before. A new McDonald's too. But there in the middle of the block was Odile's bar, same as always.

Well, I thought, memory lane, and I parked and walked in. Back in the day I used to eat lunch at Odile's all the time. Inside Odile's was familiar but different. The pinball machine was gone, replaced by a couple of video poker machines behind a plywood barrier and a sign prohibiting anyone less than eighteen to enter. An old guy was shoving nickels into one and a teenager with a bunch of tattoos was playing the other one.

There were new tables and a new menu. It looked like it was trying for something a little more upscale. But there was still a basket of saltines on the table and another basket of little jelly packets. Also ketchup, mustard, mayo and Tabasco as well as salt, pepper, and a little ceramic container of Sweet & Low. Each table had four paper placemats printed with a map of the town in the middle and little ads for local businesses around the outside: Johnny's Conoco, Ed Hebert's Allstate Insurance, C'est Si Bon Ladies Boutique, Sit and Trim Beauty Parlor and Barber Shop. On the walls were posters and schedules for the New Orleans Saints and the LSU Tigers as well as Nicholls State and the University of Louisiana Lafayette and the local high school. The floor was sticky. The ceiling fans hummed.

The waitress brought me a big plastic menu. That was new. In the old days they just put up the three or four choices on a chalk board. I noticed there was a section on the menu called "Local Favorites" as if they hoped to get some tourists here. The special of the day was crawfish étouffée. I asked if Ida May was still cooking here but the waitress, an overweight teenager, just said, "Who?" She didn't know any Ida May.

The étouffée was good and the bill came to seven dollars and twenty-six cents with sweet tea, banana pudding and tax. Not sixty-five cents like I remembered, but still pretty cheap. I wanted to ask where everything was, where the town was, the town I remembered, but I didn't know where to start so I just left a two dollar tip and walked on outside.

I got into my car and drove on out to Antoine's shack, reminder of the stupidest thing I ever did in my life. I wanted to see the place. I don't know. I wanted to see it. I don't know how it happened, but I got a little lost. There was a new subdivision outside of town. In fact, there were several. The houses looked prosperous, not outrageous rich, but prosperous. They all backed up to Bayou Coeur and some of them had swimming pools and hot tubs. Who were these people who lived in these houses?

Everything looked different, but after awhile I managed to find Antoine's shack by pure dumb luck. I drove on up to it on the shell drive that was barely visible through the weeds and I parked. The place gave off a smell, something like mildew, something like rust. I knew no one was around but I yelled out anyway, "Anybody home?" There was only a screen door hanging by a single hinge. Somebody must have stolen the old solid cypress door. I heard a rustling and the bugs scattered on the porch.

Inside the place was covered with mud. There was a big hole in the roof and pools of water had rotted the floor. Bits of metal and wood and remnants of what used to be something useful were scattered all over the four rooms. Now they were unrecognizable except for a doll's head, its hair gone, staring up at me from what used to be the bedroom floor.

A lizard looked at me from the window sill. He puffed out his red throat in a threatening display, but then decided I was too big for him and he scurried outside through a crack in the wall. "That was another life," I thought, "that was another me."

Back in the day, the boom days, that one night like most nights when I wasn't on the rig I was in T-Bob's drinking beer and playing pool. I'm one of those guys who if I played pool every day of my life I'd never get any better. I'm OK. I'm even pretty good. But some of those old boys were whizzes. Never practiced, just played. And they were good. They weren't hustlers or anything. They came right out and told you, "Twenty dollars says I can whip your ass" and if you were dumb enough to say "You're on" you were out twenty bucks.

But I was pretty good and sometimes I'd get lucky and I never bet more than I could afford to lose, so I did all right. Sometimes there'd be fights but I never got involved in that and besides everybody there liked me. Plus they knew most of the time I was good for a game and most of the time I'd have to pay up. But one night I was hot. I was really hot. I was putting down balls all over the place and making impossible massé shots and combinations and everyone was cheering me on and this guy I didn't know, had never seen him, was watching me and he challenged me to a game and he wasn't very good, I could tell that right away, but he was one of those guys who thinks he can do no wrong. You know what I mean. He'd smack every ball hard as he could, even when it didn't make sense. More than once his ball would pop back out when a softer stroke would have sunk it. But he never learned. People like that never do.

To this day I can't tell you why I did it, but I let him win. I let him crow and brag and all and all I said was "Nice game" so, of course, he upped the ante and asked me, "Care to play for some real money?" and I pretended to be reluctant, you know, and he got on me, called me a pussy and all that and so finally I said "OK. How much?" and he said "C note" and I said "OK. Rack 'em" and I just about ran the table. He got two balls and when I put away the eight ball he had to hear all the razzing from everybody else. Not me though. All I said was, "Double or nothing?" and he said "You're on."

I won that one too and he said. "I'm done," and he pulled out a hundred dollar bill and a bunch of smaller ones and all he had was about a hundred eighty-seven dollars. I told him that was fine, we're even, but he said no, he was going back home to get the rest and I said that was not necessary and he said yes it was, he paid his bills and did I want to come with him and I said no, that was OK and he said he had got cold beer and I said, well OK then and we walked out of T-Bob's and I followed his pickup out of town and we pulled into Antoine's shack. That's where he lived.

By this time it was not too late, maybe midnight, something like that, but when we pulled in I could hear a baby crying.

"Shit," said the guy, "Kid's awake."

The inside of that shack was something. There was one broken down couch and a couple straight chairs. There was no electricity, just kerosene lamps and when we walked in a woman was walking a baby up and down.

"Baby's got colic," she said and he said, "This here's a friend of mine. You got thirteen dollars?"

The woman looked at me and I could see that she was a real beauty. What was she doing there in that shack with that loser?

"Bourré or pool?" she asked.

"Pool," I said.

"Figures," she said. "Saltine tin. There's maybe twenty dollars in there."

"Listen," I said, "I don't want…."

"I owe you thirteen dollars," the man said and he looked at me hard, warning me not to show him any pity. He sure as hell did not want any of that.

"OK," I said.

The baby was quiet then and the woman said, "I'm going to bed."

The man went into the next room, the kitchen, and in a moment he returned with a five dollar bill and eight ones. He counted out the bills and then handed me a beer bottle. It was warm.

"For the road," he said and I knew he wanted me to go and so I did.

Next time I was off the rig I went to a dance—what they call a *fais do do*—at the Sugar Cane lounge. What you've got to understand about these *fais do dos* is that everyone goes. Old people. Young people. Whole families. Kids too. The older kids dance. The young ones fall asleep on a couple chairs put together by their parents. Grandpas dance with their granddaughters. Everyone goes. It's not just a rough crowd.

So I was at the dance and I saw the woman from Antoine's shack. She was sitting with a little boy on her lap, maybe two or three years old, and a baby was sleeping on a palette she made up under the table. She was bouncing the little boy on her lap and singing along with the music, some chanky-chank Cajun thing and the little boy was laughing.

I went over to her and said hi. She smiled up at me, didn't recognize me at first, then said, "Oh yeah. Pool player. Won thirteen dollars off my husband."

I didn't tell her it was two hundred. I just smiled and asked, "Where is he?"

"Probably passed out. Who knows? He left about an hour ago."

"You need a partner for a dance?"

"I got me a partner," she said, nodding toward the little boy.

"Bring him along too," I said. I held out my hand. And she took it.

The three of us waltzed around the floor and she sang along with the band, "*J'ai passé devant ta porte.*" She had beautiful, long black hair and the biggest brown eyes I have ever seen. "*J'ai crié, bye-bye ma belle.*" She smiled the whole time we were dancing. "*Il n'ya personne qui ma repondu.*" My hand circled her waist, rested on the swelling of her hip. "*Oh yai yai mon coeur fait mal.*"

I stayed with her for the next two hours. The little boy went to sleep. We danced, both of us smiling during the waltzes, both of us laughing during the two steps. After about half an hour I rested my cheek against hers during the waltzes. Another half hour and she rested her head on my shoulder.

We talked. I worked up the courage and finally asked her what I wanted to know. "Is your husband ever mean to you?" and she said "sometimes." And "Are you happy?" and she laughed as if happiness was something she couldn't imagine, but then she said the most wonderful thing any woman has ever said to me. She said, "I'm happy right now."

One more dance and her husband staggered in and he was none too happy to see me with his wife. I know this kind of people. I know how they are. Mostly they're selfish. But what little part of them isn't selfish is taken up with stupid. He walks out on his wife, leaves her with the babies, gets drunk and then he's mad because someone else pays some attention to her. What the hell did he expect?

But he was also sly, so at first he just grinned and said, "Taking care of my wife for me? That's kindly of you. Let me buy you a beer." And he went off and came back with one beer and next thing I knew I was on the floor and the music stopped and someone screamed and I realized he'd hit me on the head with the bottle. I tried to get up, but she was there standing over me and saying, "No, no, you just stay there," but I got up anyway and there was blood in my eyes and he hit me again and I was on the floor again and this time I stayed down.

I heard him yelling at her and she was yelling right back. The little boy started crying and a couple big old boys were telling him he had to leave and he was badmouthing them but you could tell he was going to do what they said. And there she was, squatting down under the table to get her baby who was still asleep and she looked over at me and she said "You don't know nothing, do you?" and then she smiled at me and said "Thanks for the dance." Then they were gone.

Somebody took me to the hospital. I had twelve stitches and three weeks later I was on a plane to Chicago to graduate school where I met my wife and then my job in New Mexico and I had my kids and now here I am visiting Antoine's shack again and thinking about that woman. I know she divorced the asshole, but after that, what?

My life in New Mexico is good. Family. Job. It's all good. Six years go by and it was my wife who suggested we take a vacation to New Orleans. She wanted to go to Jazz Fest. I say good. It'll be fun. The kids will love it. But while we're there I want to visit Bayou Coeur.

My wife and I have a great relationship. We're not only husband-wife and lovers but we're best friends. We've told each other everything about ourselves. Family. Past lovers, old romances, sex life. Everything. I've told her lots of stories about Bayou Coeur. Odile's. T-Bob's. The guys on the rigs. But for some reason I never told her about Antoine's shack and the woman who lived there. I don't know why. It's a memory just for me. It's some kind of alternate universe. Something like that anyway. Now I have plenty of common sense. Lots of it. It's kept me out of trouble, kept me from going over the deep end, stuff like that. Even that night at the *fais do do* I knew, I knew absolutely with my common sense: This is a married woman. She has two children. She is uneducated. She is nothing like you. She would probably make you very, very unhappy. But at that moment with my hand on her waist and her cheek on my cheek it was only a beer bottle on the side of my head that woke me up. Still, I like to remember that *fais do do*.

So we went to Jazz Fest and we had a great time and I rented a car and we drove west to Lafayette on the interstate and then we headed out toward Bayou Coeur. We ate at Odile's and my wife loved it. My two boys loved it. Then I drove out of town and showed them the cane fields and the new developments and we passed Antoine's shack and I watched it, I looked at it as long as I could, even catching a glimpse in my rear view mirror, but I didn't say anything about it.

That night there was a *fais do do* in Lafayette and we took the kids. There they all were just like I remembered. Old people. Teenagers. Young families. Babies sleeping under the table and on chairs put together. The band played two-steps and waltzes, about three to one, fast to slow. I taught my wife the steps. She was a fast learner. We all had a great time and after a long fast one I was sweating and out of breath and ready for a rest and a beer, but then the band struck up a waltz, a song I knew, and I just had to dance again with my wife, feel her cheek against mine, place my hand on her waist, her hip, whisper into her ear the words of the song, "*J'ai passé devant ta porte.*" She was surprised I knew the words and in French too. "*J'ai crié bye bye, ma belle.*" She looked at me in wonder. Who is this man? This father of her children. "*Il n'ya personne qui ma repondu.*" I was crying and she was alarmed. "*Oh yai yai, mon coeur fait mal.*"

That night in a hotel bed in Lafayette, our sons asleep in the bed beside us, my wife and I lay beside each other and I told her the story of Antoine's shack and the beautiful woman at the *fais do do*. She said, "I always wondered where you got that scar. I didn't want to ask."

I looked at her. She was new. She was different. Do I know this woman? I told her, "I love you," and she touched the side of my head, in the hairline above my left ear, the scar that you have to search for to see, barely visible, but still there.

DECISION TREE

Jerry thought he would get a cold one, a quick cold one in an air-conditioned bar, and then head home. It was seven o'clock, his tie was at half mast and he carried his suit coat flung over his arm, the arm that held the brief case which contained the stuff for the meeting tomorrow that he needed to look at but knew he wouldn't. There was a ballgame on TV tonight that he wanted to see. There were acceptable take out leftovers in the fridge. But first a quick cold one.

For quick cold ones he preferred a hotel bar. For one thing they were rarely crowded at this hour. For another they were clean, well appointed, efficient, usually had bowls of tasty snacks and some effort at décor. Also if there were any customers at all at this early hour they more than likely would be travelers, tourists, people he just might want to talk to. If he cared to admit it, pretty women all dolled up for a night on the town, hopeful, maybe in the mood to meet a handsome stranger in a distant town, especially the distant town of New Orleans. If not, there was always the TV turned to sports.

He walked into the almost empty bar and registered with satisfaction that it was cool—very cool. Instantly the sweat dried on his armpits. It was even cool enough to put his jacket back on. He felt refreshed. Ah. He wondered what was on draft.

After the beer arrived and he had a long refreshing quaff and two fistfuls of salty peanuts he looked around. Aha. There, seated at a booth all alone and lovely was a young woman, long dark brown, almost black hair, pale skin, deep red lips. She wore a simple but elegant dress also red that complemented her lips. She was, of course, sipping a cool white wine.

Jerry got up and carried his beer to her booth. She looked up with something like excitement or perhaps alarm, but managed a small inquisitive smile.

"Hi. My name is Jerry. Mind if I join you?"

She cocked her head in an appraising manner.

"That's it? You don't have some line?"

"Nope. No line."

"Why not? You don't know any lines?"

"Lines are just something to say before you say 'Hi, my name is Jerry. Mind if I join you?'"

"Yeah, but isn't that the whole purpose of a line? Something that will induce the girl to say yes?"

"No line has ever done that."

"You think so?"

"I know so. So do you. A guy comes up to the table. Before he even opens his mouth you already know whether you're going to say yes or no. Sometimes it's yes and it gets changed to a no because the line is just too stupid or corny to bear, but no no has ever— ever in the history of the world—become a yes because of anything the guy says."

"So you skip the line."

"Yeah, I skip the line. I figure you're either open to somebody—anybody—sitting down—or maybe you're open to me in particular to sitting down—or you're not and nothing I say is going to make any difference."

"So cut to the chase?"

"Right."

"You that way about everything?"

"No. I can be as conventional as the next guy. And patient too."

"But really don't you just want to get into my pants?"

"Is that an accusation or an invitation?"

She almost choked on her wine, which she had raised to her lips in an elegant and sophisticated gesture. She was laughing, usually a good sign, unless of course the laughter was at his expense.

"And would your answer be different if it was one or the other?" she asked coyly, sipping again, although the gesture had lost some of its panache.

"Of course. If it's an accusation I say no. If it's an invitation I say yes."

"So insincerity is not out of the question."

"Oh no, I'm very sincere."

"Lying then."

"Not lying. Rolling with the punches."

"Saying what I want to hear."

"No. Not even that. Just making the usual harmless pretenses."

"And what might those be?"

"Well, pretending, for example, that a date—any date—no matter how casual—isn't in some way an audition."

"That's good."

"It's a commonplace."

"I suppose so. So you always want sex?"

"Every man does. And most women too."

"I read somewhere that men think about sex every seven seconds."

"Very true."

"Really?"

"Really."

"How do you get any work done?"

"Here's how it works. You've heard, I suppose, that the brain is always thinking about something. You can't think of nothing."

"Uh-huh."

"OK. In the case of women, your brains think about all sorts of things—who knows what. In the case of men, all we ever think about is sex—but if we concentrate our minds on something else—no problem—we can think about that—we can even think for seven seconds or seven minutes or seven hours about that something—but we have to be *actively* thinking—really concentrating, you know. The second we let our mind wander—bang!—we're at our default setting—and our default setting is always sex."

"Default setting. I bet you work in computers."

"No. I use them, but who doesn't?"

"So what do you do?"

"If we're going to have a conversation, why not have it at eye level? I could sit down."

She was very, very beautiful. Jerry had always made it a policy to admire the very, very beautiful women from afar. If he was going to hit on somebody, he'd choose the pretty girl on the other side of the room, the miss congeniality of the group, the second runner-up.

He had never had much success with the very, very beautiful. Of course, he could be wrong. She was, after all, benefiting from the advantage of being the most beautiful girl in the room and might slip down a notch or two if the place filled up with other candidates. She also was the only girl in the room.

She really did remind him of Ruth and that was a bit disconcerting. They both favored dramatically red lipstick. There was something in the way she crinkled her eyes too or maybe he was imagining that. He had found himself finding superficial reminders of Ruth in other women for the last six months and upon further review always realized he had been wrong. Ruth was only in his head, she wasn't out there in other women. Not really.

At one time he had thought Ruth was the one for him, the one who would share his life. There was the usual euphoria, the passion that did not allow for anything like thoughtful analysis or sensible caution. But even after that passed, they seemed to get along so well. Everyone said so. "Such a cute couple." "You're made for each other." That sort of thing. In another time, another age, they would have already been married. If they had grown up on adjacent farms, were stuck by fate and geography and habit, they'd not only already be married but have at least one or two of their eventual brood of children. But times change and people change and opportunities arise and decisions are made and then things happen. Like that. So Ruth was in San Antonio with her fabulous opportunity that was after all just a job and here he was in New Orleans with his career where he had to be and unlucky for him Ruth found someone else close to home while Jerry was negotiating their long distance romance and trying to balance their desires and that was more or less that. He moved on, that's for sure, but no one else had managed to make him forget her and now here was this beautiful woman and damned if she didn't remind him of Ruth. His luck she'll be from Oklahoma and going back home tomorrow where her high school sweetheart waits. Something like that anyway.

But wait a minute. Who cares, right? Ball game/roll in the hay. Ball game/roll in the hay. We're not talking a life altering decision here. It's a pretty girl, that's all. Sit down, have a beer, see if anything develops. That's all.

She was looking at him with a frank, perhaps even exaggerated sense of appraisal, trying to make it attractive, sexy, but still in control.

"Hmm. I haven't decided yet."

He smiled ruefully. "Ah. So it's going to be an interview?"

"Do you mind some impertinent questions?"

"Fire away?"

"Any STDs or SOs?"

"No STDs. What's an SO?

"Significant other."

"Ah. No. Well, strictly speaking, yes, perhaps not in the way you mean it, but of course there are others who are significant. But no—I am not—attached. Not diseased. Not attached."

"I can see you are gainfully employed."

"Yes."

"I don't suppose you live with your parents?"

"No."

"Divorced?"

"No."

"Politics? Religion? Thoughts about kids? Oh, number of siblings?"

"I am a bleeding heart liberal, raised Catholic, born again agnostic-humanist, I hope to have children, two maybe three if the first two are the same sex—I'd like to have at least one of each. I have one sister. You?"

"You don't care about me."

"I do."

"You don't care about the answer to any of those questions."

"I do."

"No you don't or you would have asked them."

"I would have asked them eventually, just like eventually you'd get around to deciding about whether or not you wanted to have sex with me. We care about the same things, just not in the same order."

"So I'll only have sex with lapsed Catholic liberal-humanists who like kids and have one sister?"

"No, but you'd definitely reject a Southern Baptist neo-conservative with twelve siblings."

She laughed. "OK."

"OK. I can sit down?"

"OK, you're right. A couple more questions."

He sighed, but the fact is he was enjoying this. He leaned against the wall, sipped his beer. She was enjoying it too, enjoying the power, the upper hand she had in this game. She set down her wine, but continued to hold the stem in her hand, careful not to warm the cooling liquid that was beading on the outside of the glass.

"OK. If I say yes, if you sit down, how do you perceive the rest of the evening going? What is your plan?"

It was true that she had hoped for something just like this to happen. Why else had she dressed so carefully, taken so much care with her makeup and hair? Used that little bit more of perfume? Felt the tinge of disappointment when she entered the hotel bar and found it empty? Felt the tiny surge of excitement when the handsome stranger entered the bar, obviously a local, suit coat flung over his arm, toting a briefcase, sweating and tired from a day of work.

So what was on tap? What would be the program with this guy? She was guessing something perfect. He was considering her question, how to answer it, what goodies to promise to get her to agree. He cleared his throat.

Jerry smiled. "You ever hear of a decision tree?"

"No."

"OK. First step is simple. I sit down. I order two more drinks. That ensures that we'll be here together for awhile. We talk and because we're both strangers we ask polite questions. I'll want to know if you're only in town for awhile or you live here. First decision tree. If you live here—well, that sets up certain possibilities. You're just in town until tomorrow—well, that eliminates certain possibilities. You see?"

"Yes."

"OK. Then other talk. Do *you* have any significant others? Why are you here? What were your plans for the evening? Have you eaten yet? Decision tree."

"I get it. You know a little place."

"Right. Actually I know dozens of places, some of them not so little. I suggest some place or give you a few choices."

"Do you like Cajun food?"

He laughs. "Yeah. Like that. All of these places will have one thing in common."

"What's that?"

"They're nice, the food is good, and they're not so fancy or expensive that it looks like I'm trying to impress you."

"Slick."

"Right. OK. Decision tree. Your decision this time. You figure all in all you don't want to spend the rest of the evening with me—you tell me you already ate or you have a late dinner date with someone else or whatever and we amicably finish our drinks and I take off. *Or* you say 'Yeah, I'd love to try some Cajun food, is it anything like Thai?' and we go off to eat."

"Is Cajun food anything like Thai?"

"Not a bit."

She laughs again, enjoying this.

"OK" Jerry says, pulling his tie, "let's say you decide to take the culinary plunge. We take a taxi, we continue to talk. We're at the restaurant—not Cajun—New Orleans has the best food in the world—and we continue to talk. There will be at least three courses— salad, entrée, dessert—a set of time that means we have to be together. What will happen? We hit if off or we find ourselves bored or shy or intimidated or who knows. Maybe we feel like soul mates, maybe we're thrilled. Maybe we're praying for the coffee to arrive. What happens, end of dinner...."

"Decision tree."

"Right. This time I get to choose first."

"You do?"

"Sure. I either take you home or I say something like 'You like jazz?'"

"You know this little place."

"I know a dozen little places, not all jazz."

"I like jazz. Besides, this is New Orleans. You have to hear some jazz."

"Good."

"But maybe I'll be too tired."

"Decision tree."

"Right. So then let's say—I'm always taking the decision tree direction with the best possible outcome."

"Of course."

"For illustrative purposes only."

"Of course. Of course."

"Let's hurry through the next steps."

"OK"

"Jazz. Late night drink. Holding hands. A sweet kiss. Growing intimacy. We've shared some pretty private thoughts. You come back to my place."

"I do?"

"Or we go to yours."

"Possible."

"There's something terribly appropriate on the stereo."

"Barry Manilow?"

"You're kidding."

"Yes." She laughed.

"Thank God. OK. We dance, because of course that's easier than just throwing ourselves into each other's arms. OK?"

"Decision tree."

"Right."

"I get to decide this one."

"I know. I know."

"You, of course, want sex, you always want sex."

"Of course."

"So I get to decide."

"Right. So going with the program let's say…."

"But what if I never—I mean never on the first date…."

"That's cool."

"It is?"

"Sure. I make another date. Maybe a ballgame for tomorrow. Day game. At 1 p.m. And I can snag tickets for…."

"Wait a minute. What if I say yes?"

"Well, in that case…let's hope ecstasy."

"Wow."

"Right. And then sweet sleep."

"You stay over?"

"If you want."

"Decision tree."

"Right. And breakfast. And then…I'm still thinking ball game. We're inseparable, we become an item, engaged, married, have 2.5 kids, live happily ever after. Something like that anyway."

"Or?"

"Or I finish this beer, go home and watch the ballgame on TV. Or I sit down, we have a couple drinks and then I go home. Or we go out to eat and then I go home. Or everything happens like before except we get bored with each other six months from now and we break up. Or maybe two weeks before our twentieth wedding anniversary you run away with your tennis instructor or…."

"I get it. Decision tree."

"Right. So. The time has come."

"What time?"

"Time for the first decision. Hi my name is Jerry. Mind if I join you?"

She looked up at him expectantly. Her fingers rolled around the vanishing coolness from her glass. He was pretending to be cool and above it all, but she knew that if she said no, he would be disappointed although he would do his best to hide it. So much need. So much need.

Jerry was aware as he had been all along from the time he leaned against the wall that he could see deep down the cleavage of that spectacular dress and just make out the edges of her little pink nipple. He figured if he left now he'd be home in time for the third inning. His stomach growled. All this talk of nice little restaurants, no way was he going to be satisfied with the left over take out. He'd have to pick something up. He thought about breakfast, the kind of breakfast the two of them would share if they woke in tumbled sheets and a kind of surprised happiness. He decided he was going to suggest some bistro food. *Moules frites.* Very tasty. Very sexy.

She knew, of course, that he was looking at her breasts. Why else had she worn this particular dress? Why was she oh so casually leaning forward to offer him a better view? Why then did it bother her? Would she feel better if he averted his gaze? And he was after all very good at pretending not to care so much. Oh, but he did care. His care was a hunger, a hunger for her, which she found very exciting, satisfying, and a little scary. She began to feel lucky she now knew a local who could take her out to some place the tourists didn't know about.

Only a second had gone by. They were both smiling. Jerry wondered what the coolest thing he could do was. Hang on and wait? Say something devastatingly perfect? What would that be? "Time's up? Have a nice evening?" And then drain his beer and walk out, ears cocked for a possible "Wait." That would be cool. Either way he had his dignity.

How about—"OK. I'm deciding." Then sit down. That would get the program rolling. It would show he was a man of action. But really, didn't it also admit defeat? Was it an act of desperation? Too much need?

She was thinking, when we're old and our grandchildren ask how we met will I be able to tell them what I'm thinking now? And she really liked the way he looked in that suit. Some guys look terrible in a suit. He looked good.

He had shifted his gaze from the now obscured nipple (since she was leaning back) to the exquisite thigh revealed in her crossed legs and her no doubt very expensive shoes. But he also had to return to that adorable face, the dark hair, pale skin, red lips that he had always liked. And what a smile. She was a dazzler.

In her purse were the two tickets to the very popular, hard to get show that she was longing to see. The two tickets were one for her and one for Tom, ordered months ago with such excitement, but of course now Tom wasn't here, he'd stayed home pleading economy, pleading work, pleading, pleading and the plan had been she would sell or at the very least give away the ticket to some deserving fellow conventioneer, certainly female in Tom's mind, but she had had no luck at selling and was insufficiently motivated to give the damned ticket away and now it sat, valuable piece of cardboard in her purse. Should she offer it to this handsome stranger? But of course that was not what he had in mind. A show. No. That wasn't it at all. It wouldn't tempt him away from his ballgame. Of course he might say yes in hopes of after theater frolicking, but that would put him in an antsy and foul mood, sure to make him hypercritical of the fluffy over priced tourist entertainment he would have to endure in order to get on with the program. Was she willing to forego these very expensive tickets for a who knows what evening? And what would she tell Tom—as if she cared much now that he had shown himself so...so...well, Tom was already history in her mind. It would serve him right if the tickets lay unused in her purse or perhaps she could bestow them on the bartender or on some complete strangers...a middle aged couple on the street who would be suspicious but thrilled.

This man, Jerry he said his name was, he seems very nice. And wouldn't it be pleasant to spend an evening at a little restaurant—it was odd how she—you—anyone—always thought of such things as "little" restaurant—exquisite food, some obvious regulars, a mom and pop establishment full of love and devotion and expertise, not to mention a terrific wine list. The desserts wouldn't tempt them. He would suggest somewhere else, a place he knew that made all their concoctions in house. A real find. No one knew about it yet. Everyone knew. Delicious. She noticed with satisfaction that he was tall, tall enough for her 5'9" frame that really insisted—she knew it was being superficial, but still the heart knows what it wants—that really insisted on a man whose shoulder was high enough to provide a comfy cushion for her head. You could dance with this guy. She hoped he liked dancing.

Jerry could tell that she was tall. Even sitting down she looked tall, long waisted, long legged, long hair even that went with the whole package. If the truth be told even her nose was a bit long. But on her it worked. He was betting she was a conventioneer, here in town for a few days. As if to confirm this a gaggle of people all dressed for the evening but still bearing convention badges entered laughing into the bar and she glanced at them first with concern and then with relief that she didn't know any of them. They sat at a table and laughed and talked loudly and yes, there peeking out of her open purse was a brightly colored lanyard that no doubt held her credentials, perhaps a presenter or officer at the event. She uncrossed her leg revealing a wide swath of thigh and switching legs, crossed them again, demurely but ineffectively tugging at the hem of her beautiful red dress. Was that an innocent gesture or was it meant for him? He was hoping she was not a tease even as he registered pleasure in the teasing, intended or accidental.

And still they waited. Really. Really, really they knew absolutely nothing about each other, nothing important anyway. He didn't know that those expensive shoes were the only expensive shoes she had ever bought in her life and that it still made her sick to think how much she had paid for them.

She didn't know that he hated shaving and in exactly two weeks he would decide to grow a beard, which he would keep the rest of his life. Neither one of them knew anything, but they continued to smile.

"Well," she said.

He cocked an eyebrow in what he supposed was a hopeful but still cool manner.

"Well," she said again, "Do you believe in brutal honesty?"

"No. I believe in kindness."

"Me too."

"On the other hand…."

"Yes, I know, you like to know where you stand, you like to look ahead and see how the decision tree is likely to go two or three steps down the road."

"One or two anyway."

"Yeah. I can relate to that."

He looked at his watch.

"You have somewhere to go?"

"No. Brutal honesty?"

"Just this once."

"If I strike out here, I'm headed home to watch a ballgame. It already started."

"So you'd like to know…well, if all you're going to get is another half hour and a beer or two here with me, all in all you'd rather not miss the ballgame."

"Brutal honesty?"

"Sure. One more time."

"Yes."

"I suppose you know all the best Cajun and Creole restaurants, right?"

"Yeah, I do, but I prefer bistro food."

"Really?"

"Yeah. *Cassoulet. Choucroute. Boeuf Bourguinon. Pot au feu. Moules frites.*"

"I love *moules frites.*"

"Really?"

"Yeah."

They smiled, but she realized that the dynamics were changing. Before had been playful and there was so much pleasure for both of them in the sweet uncertainty and the anticipation, but now she held all the power and in a moment he would resent her for it no matter what she said. He didn't know it yet, but soon he would be compelled to show her, to wrest some control, maybe need it enough to walk away and go to his damned ballgame.

It was true. He was beginning to lose patience. Did he really want to stand there and be judged? He finished his beer. It was time.

Jerry blinked. For an instant the woman's beauty disappeared. For an instant—the instant of the blink—he felt a surge of anger. Why was he in this position? Why was he allowing himself to be judged? Appraised? Evaluated? Why was he putting up with this? Why had he arrived, a humble supplicant at the feet of the female to be so dispassionately, so coldly, so selfishly rendered into one of two camps—acceptable or not? What he should do is turn and walk out of here, walk out and hail a cab and head for the airport, give up everything in a grand and final gesture, everything of his laughably successful life and fly to San Antonio and carry off Ruth to a cheap motel and start a new life doing anything—selling shoes, doing construction, maybe becoming an athletic trainer like he once had dreamed. His eyes flicked open. An athletic trainer? Cheap hotel? What the hell is wrong with him? He remembered the meeting with Ralph and Tina and Curtis that awaited in the morning. He looked at the girl who was still beautiful and was now smiling, friendly, really, nothing of the cold umpire, everything of the friendly co-conspirator, enjoying harmlessly this moment of flirtation. He could understand that. He noticed her dimple. He could live with that dimple for the rest of his life, pass it on to their children, cuddle for long hours after the kids went to bed, share, share everything. She really was adorable. What would she say next?

She was realizing that he was probably just a bit older than she had first realized. This did not matter or if it mattered it was a plus, she was after all rather attracted to older men and anyway he wasn't really old, just not young and unformed. She was betting his apartment was neat and clean, not the dorm like mess that attended so many of her past younger boy friends, the clueless receding into history Tom. And he was handsome that's for sure. Not movie star looks or anything, but good looking. She noticed again that he was tall and she thought about how her head would feel on that shoulder.

She wondered: what was the perfect thing to say. He wondered: what was the perfect thing to do.

The bartender switched the TV to the game. There is a man on second. Two outs. The count is two and two. The catcher puts down the sign. The pitcher nods, pauses, looks over his shoulder to second. He rocks and delivers. The runner takes off. The batter swings.

THE NEXT MORNING

The next morning Tommy was up early. The girl was still asleep in his bed. He stood in his living room facing his stereo and tried to remember her name. He thought it might start with a B. An old fashioned name. Beatrice? Bianca? He ran his fingers along the cds that ranged across the shelves that took up half of the wall between the front windows and the arch going into the kitchen He had not planned to touch them all. It was an idle gesture, a caress really, a gesture of affection and he had only meant to sustain the touch for a moment. But once started he somehow and for some inexplicable reason felt compelled to continue or rather having started, he could think of no good reason to stop. His finger traveled every spine of every cd, moving left to right, down a shelf, then right to left and so on until he had touched them all.

Tommy had known for some time that cds were doomed and soon all the music he would ever want, all the music in the world would be available in the aptly named cloud and he could access it all with nothing more than a small flat device not much bigger than the plastic card that could access money. The problem was he enjoyed buying cds. He enjoyed picking them up in a store, reading the titles and the tracks, making choices, carrying them home, shedding the cellophane and placing them lovingly on his sturdy and useful machine that then played them aloud. Magic. Music appeared in the air. Now he needed only the air.

Except it wasn't true. Someone somewhere had a physical something that contained the music and he would no longer have a physical something, but only an intangible and much less satisfying thing—access. Still, it was music and Tommy recognized the superiority of the new order as well as its inevitability, just as he had recognized the no longer relevant tapes that were still present but hidden on the shelves behind his cds.

He could, of course, simply chuck the cds, bite the bullet, go online and download everything he needed, but it made financial sense to convert these cds, to translate their music into whatever it was that could fit into the cloud. He had finally decided that that was exactly what he was going to do. But after a mere hour of tackling the job he learned that the process was just short enough to allow for nothing else but just long enough to be annoying. He had many hundreds of cds, probably approaching a thousand. It was going to take him forever or at least enough time that he couldn't imagine doing it.

The answer, of course, was obvious. There were plenty of geeks who would be more than willing to do the job for him—for a price, a price that would no doubt make the whole process not much cheaper than just chucking them all in the first place.

He heard the toilet flush. The girl was up. A moment later she appeared in the archway. Her eyes were red and her hair was tousled. "Good morning," she said, "what time is it?"

"Almost eight."

"Why are you up so early?"

"I have to work."

"Oh."

"You want breakfast?"

She made a face. "No, I couldn't eat a thing."

"There's coffee."

"Ah."

"In the kitchen. Cups are left of the stove."

The girl had come to his food truck just as he was closing up. He gave her a pulled pork sandwich and asked, "Want to look around the truck?" She helped him close up and he drove her back to his apartment where she spent the night and now here she was.

When she appeared again in the doorway she was holding a coffee cup. She ran her fingers through her hair.

"I could be wrong," Tommy said, "but I don't think you ever told me your name."

"It's Monica and you're wrong. I told you." Monica. Of course. Not Beatrice. Not even a B. Monica.

"You're Tommy, right?"

"Right."

"I like your truck."

"You want a job?"

"A job?" She laughed. It was a nice laugh. She was a pretty girl. Maybe not as pretty as he had thought the night before, but she was definitely a pretty girl, a Bywater beauty, one of those hipsters who dressed in the current uniform that twenty years ago would have been the very definition of nerd but today proclaimed the kind of casual hipness that required a lot of work and care to pull off. Now, however, her hair was not just tousled just so, but definitely a case of bed head and while her mascara was still in place her lipstick had worn off and not yet been replaced. She could have used a comb and a mirror. Still, she was definitely pretty.

"A job?" she said again. "I don't think so."

"Why not?"

"I have a job."

"Oh."

She looked around the apartment. The night before there had been no chance to check it out, no preludes, no pretense of asking if she'd like a drink or anything like that. They had both known what was what and what was on the program and had gone immediately to the bedroom.

"You have a lot of cds."

"Yeah. Yes. I do."

"You should get an ipod. It's much…."

"I have an ipod."

"Oh, OK."

There was a silence. The girl again said "OK." A bird chirped and the girl pulled her cell phone out of her jeans, looked at it, poked it a few times with her fingers and put it back. "Good coffee," she said.

"Boy friend?" Tommy asked.

"My mother."

"Oh."

There was another silence. "I could call a cab," she said, "or a friend."

"No, no. I'll drive you."

"You don't have to do that."

"Didn't you leave your car…?"

"No. I was with friends."

"Oh."

"Well," she said. She was holding the cup in both her hands, warming them. She took another sip. Looked around the room, avoiding his eyes.

"I need to tell you something," he said.

"No, no," she said quickly, "no, you don't."

"I think I do."

"There's no need."

"I just got out of jail."

That stopped her. Finally, after a nervous laugh she asked, "What for?"

"Book making."

"I didn't know bookkeeping was a crime."

"Not bookkeeping. Book making. I was a bookie. I made bets for people. It's called keeping a book."

"Oh. That's illegal?"

"That and tax evasion."

"Oh, well, yeah, I guess so." Another silence. "So how long were you in?"

"Eighteen months.

"That's not so much."

Tommy thought about this. Not so much. Maybe not, but for him it had been plenty. He lost his business, the sandwich shop that was doing so well. And, of course, his book. And a year and a half of his life. When his best friend, Paul, visited him at the B.B. "Sixty" Rayburn Correctional Facility in Bogalusa the first thing Tommy told him was "Thanks, Buddy."

"For what?" Paul asked.

"For not saying I told you so."

"Hell, Tommy, you know I'm thinking it."

Tommy had laughed. Yeah. Of course Paul was thinking it. He had warned him. "You've got a good business, Tommy, a good life. Taking over a book is a big risk. You don't need it." But, of course, Tommy hadn't listened. "This is New Orleans, buddy. Everybody and his uncle gambles. And the sheriff's brother-in-law is my biggest customer. I'll be OK."

But then the old sheriff got caught up in a scandal and was forced to resign. A special election brought in a new sheriff and seven months later the new sheriff was cooperating with the feds who came knocking on Tommy's door. They arrested him first for tax evasion and then a whole list of other crimes including running an illegal book, racketeering and money laundering. Tommy copped a plea and ended up paying a big fine and spending that year and a half in Bogalusa. Not good, but maybe the girl was right.

"Yeah," Tommy said, "It could have been worse, I guess. I lost my business too."

"Your book making?"

"Well, yeah. But I also lost my restaurant."

"So now you have a food truck."

"Yeah."

"You like it though, right?"

Tommy thought about this. "Yeah. It's OK. I like it." Another silence. "Listen," he said.

"No, no," she said, "you don't have to explain. It's OK."

"No, that's not…I mean…if you want…you could spend some time with me today. On the truck I mean. Not the whole day—and I'll pay you…that's not…anyway, either way if you want I'd like to…you know, call you sometime, so if you want…you know, Monica, I'd like your phone number if you're up to seeing an ex-con and all." He laughed, hoping he was projecting an image of calm, a guy who was absolutely safe, not the sort of guy who picked up girls in his food truck and brought them home for a casual one night stand, which was, of course, exactly the kind of guy he was. She was looking embarrassed.

"Tommy," she said.

"It's OK if you don't want to."

"The thing is I have this appointment at noon."

"Lunch."

"Yes. I have this friend."

"OK." Another silence.

"You got a phone?" she asked.

"Yes."

"My number is 878-3615."

"Oh. OK." He pulled out his phone and entered the number. "878-3615, right?"

"That's it."

"So, where do you want me to drop you off?"

"You know where the Parkway is? By Bayou St. John?"

"Yes."

"Right there will be good."

"OK."

"I better get my stuff. Wash my face. You know?"

"Sure."

She went through the archway and walked toward the bedroom and bathroom. As soon as she turned the corner Tommy punched in her number on his phone and waited to hear the chirp of a bird. Instead he got a message saying "this number has been disconnected or is out of order." He composed his face in a smile.

When the girl reappeared her hair was combed and pulled into a hasty pony tail. Her purse was on her shoulder, her phone in her hand.

Tommy picked up the keys to his truck. "You ready?" he asked.

They didn't talk much on the drive. She tried to act friendly, made a few comments about his truck. He let her talk without comment. When he pulled over next to the Parkway Bakery she hesitated only for a second, then she got out calling back to him, "Thanks for the ride." Then she took off walking down the street. Tommy watched her go.

Tommy returned home late that night after a long day on the food truck. Twice he had called the girl's number just to make sure he had not made a mistake. He opened his fridge and got out a beer. When he closed the door he noticed something. On the refrigerator door he always had a small notepad of paper held with a magnet, three other magnets that were plain red dots and his favorite, the magnet he had shown Paul of the girl saying "You ever notice that 'what the hell' is always the right answer?" That magnet was missing. In its place under one of the red dots was a note:

"I stole your magnet.

Sorry. I just had to have it.

Maybe I'll return it someday.

P.S. Sorry about the phone number too.

I'm just a bitch I guess."

Tommy took his beer to his chair, sat down and turned on the TV. A ballgame was in progress. He clicked the remote to Guide and scrolled through the more than nine hundred choices for something better to watch.

AFTER THE STORM

We didn't get any flooding but we did get wind. Lots of wind. Thousands of trees and telephone poles were knocked down. One of those trees was a tall pine in the lot next door which fell on the neighbor's house, crushed the roof and kept on falling until it hit the foundation. The top of the tree missed our house by about two feet. The people next door, Charley Apple, his girlfriend Maggie, their one eyed chocolate lab and three of her puppies all survived the tree without a scratch and right in the middle of the storm, about six in the morning, they piled into their pickup and took off for Charley's mother's house out in the country. We all heard the crash and we watched the pickup turning the corner and speeding off. The sun was just coming up.

That was five years ago and Charley hasn't been back. For six months the crushed house and tree stayed there. Finally the house was torn down, the tree was cut up and all the debris was carted away. The only things that remained were the remnants of the semi-attached garage and a metal tower that in the days before the storm Charlie used as a practice deer blind. Sitting in the weeds near the dismantled tower was a brown foam deer with a bulls eye painted on its side. Charley used to sit up on that tower and shoot arrows into that foam deer.

This was a little odd for a residential street but we didn't mind. What we and the rest of the neighbors did mind was the one eyed chocolate lab who used to climb up that tower and then sit there and bark and howl because she couldn't figure out how to get down. How in the world she managed to climb the tower in the first place was a mystery, especially since she usually waited until the middle of the night when everyone was asleep.

We'd call the police and they would arrive and try to coax her down, but she was both scared and mean and no amount of coaxing worked. Where the hell Charley Apple was during all this commotion no one knew. "Just shoot the bitch," someone would say, but of course the cops couldn't do that and they would have to wait for Charley to get home.

About three months after the remains of the house were carted off, someone stole the tower and the foam deer and the next four years the garage stood empty by itself in the midst of all the weeds which eventually grew four feet and more. After unsuccessfully attempting to get Charley Apple to mow his property the city did it for him and sent him the bill. Meanwhile, Charley Apple, Maggie and the dogs were living in a double wide out on Charley's mother's property near Tickfaw and he listed his property for sale. The asking price was two hundred thirty thousand dollars, which was ridiculous. True it was a double lot, but there was no house and everyone agreed Charley was crazy if he thought anyone was going to pay that kind of money for an empty lot, even if it was a double.

I blame the storm for what happened next. I know that lots of folks blame the storm for everything and anything, but in my case I believe I'm right. I look back and try to see if there were any signs, any hint before the storm. Maybe—but really the storm was when my wife began to change.

My wife is a sweetheart (or used to be anyway) and I still love her for what was, but she's what you call agoraphobic now and for a long time her only contact with the world outside our house was what she saw through the windows and one whole fourth of what she saw was that butt ugly empty lot and that pitiful half garage. The other three sides of our house offer the following views: front side looks out on the street, our front lawn, the sidewalk, azalea bushes, a live oak, the street, the houses across the street, the occasional car. Back side, a very nice backyard, the tall fence covered with jasmine and honeysuckle vines, the loquat tree, a bed of flowers, palmettos, ornamental kale and cabbage, variegated ginger, a line of pygmy banana trees, a pitiful little satsuma tree, our vegetable garden with low lying plants: tomatoes, cucumbers, squash, radishes, bush beans in the spring; collards, cabbage, more beans, turnips in the fall. West side: the house next door, its brown cypress sides punctuated by two stories of windows and a gable, the chain link fence, a peek at their garbage cans and their standard poodle mostly sleeping on the back steps. And on the east: that ugly lot.

For a long time, I took care of the yard, front and back. I didn't really enjoy it very much. I have lots of other things I'd rather be doing, but I thought about Martha (that's my wife's name, Martha) and how the view from the windows was just about all she had left for pleasure and so I got out my gloves and my little garden stool and I got to work. After awhile the place looked really nice.

The thing is I am thorough. I made some raised beds, put up railroad ties and dug deep, really deep down to the clay and then I sieved that dirt, really broke it up, filtered out all the pebbles and roots and I mixed in sand and manure, fertilizer and top soil, really worked that soil until it was perfect. I planned to do the same thing all along the backyard fence line where I have the loquat and the banana trees and the satsuma. They're doing OK, but all around them is a mixture of various sickly flowers and an abundance of weeds.

I never liked working in the yard but I used to like making plans. I did research, bought books and went on the internet. I bought some graph paper and made quarter inch scale drawings, printing in the names of all the plants I planned to place, what and where, and how many. I loved making those plans. Problem is that was all I did. I must have made a dozen or more different plans, all drawn carefully on that graph paper, color coordinated, labels printed, but the plans stayed put in the second drawer of my desk.

Eventually I stopped planning. I just went on down to Lowe's or to one of the several garden centers we have here in town and I looked around and if I saw something interesting, I'd buy it and then I came home and put it down somewhere, planted it, saw what developed. There's quite a variety. I improvised. A little something here. A little something there. It all adds up. It was really coming along. There always seems to be room for one more thing. That's the way my days went. I'm retired now and have plenty of time.

Martha likes to cook. She always liked to cook, but since she developed her fear of going outside, she really expanded her repertoire. She got addicted to the food channel. It started out all she'd do was make recipe cards. She'd watch a show about one thing or another and she'd copy down the recipes and then transfer them to the cards, being careful to print them very clearly and noting on the bottom where the recipe came from.

She'd do this all day long and never have time to actually cook anything except something simple like spaghetti or red beans and rice, and of course with those there was always leftovers. But then one day she called me in to lunch and there was homemade tomato basil soup and paninis with homemade mayonnaise with garlic and tarragon. That's what started it. I went on and on about how good it was and next day for supper she made veal Marsala that was the best thing I believe I ever ate. After that every meal was something special. I guess in some ways I am a lucky man.

I wished she would go out though. I did all the shopping and the things she wanted were sometimes hard to find. Leeks for example. Anaheim chile peppers. Panko. Wasabi. Sweetbreads. Chicory. Going all over town trying to find a particular kind of olive isn't my idea of how I wanted to spend my retirement. The food was great though so I guess I shouldn't complain.

Sometimes I'd be outside in the back putting in something or other I bought at the garden center, maybe some more pansies or that line of irises I put in behind the vegetable garden where they can get their feet wet like they like and I'd look up and see Martha sitting at the kitchen table watching me through the window. She has her binoculars which she used to look at the birds, and her little life list bird book where she notes down all the species she sees. But I knew she wasn't looking at birds. She was looking at me. She imagined I was enjoying myself and she wished she could be out there with me getting her hands dirty, feeling the soil, making little holes in the earth and burying bulbs that will come up with color and wouldn't that be something? But she can't. It was all she could muster just to sit on the front porch and hope no neighbor stopped by to say hello. Or opened the screen door and still standing on the porch, she reached around to the mailbox once the mailman left and she retrieved the usual bills and ads and magazines. Even to step out on that front step was too much for her. It got to be pretty extreme. I started hoping she wouldn't close the blinds and the drapes and cut herself off even from the sight of the world outside the house. I've read up on agoraphobia and I know that happens sometimes.

When we ate dinner, the conversation was lively. She followed all the news and had definite political opinions. She liked sports too and lived and died for LSU and the Saints. She knew all the players, their numbers, where they came from, their stats. I'm a fan too but she had all the facts, so when she criticized the coach for a play call, I generally agreed. She said she'd love to go to the Superdome and I tried to push this, hoping it would be a catalyst to getting her out. We could go with friends. We could tail gate. She even suggested menus for the tailgating. I encouraged all this, but all she said was "Maybe next year, you know I can't do that now. Not really."

It was gradual. The agoraphobia. "Can you run to the store for me, honey?" "Oh, I don't like to go to that old movie theater. We can get movies delivered right to the door. I'll make popcorn. Let's stay home." She'd go outside to get the paper and hurry back in. She'd wait for the mailman to leave and then go outside to get the mail, holding the screen door open behind her. She waited too long to renew her driver's license and couldn't do it by mail and I realized she hadn't been in the car for months. Finally she couldn't put it off and she ran out of excuses and I drove her to the DMV. In the parking lot outside the office she began hyperventilating and then crying, pleading with me, "Just wait a minute. Just wait. I'll be OK." She finally went in, holding my hand in a death grip and got through the questions and the eye exam. I had to let go of her hand to pay the fee and she grabbed my arm and I could smell the sweat, the fear in her, could see her red face, the tight line of her mouth, the trembling of the fingers pressing into my arm.

When I got her back home, we sat in the kitchen and I poured her a glass of iced tea and she kept saying over and over, "I am so sorry. You poor man. You poor man. I am so sorry. You just don't know." That was two years ago and she hasn't been out of the house since. At first she would be OK with the yard, especially the back yard which was more or less enclosed, but eventually even that was too much and she stayed in the house, completely in the house and I didn't know what to do.

For awhile I lied to our friends, made excuses when they invited us to something or other, but eventually I had to tell them the truth. Her best friend, Gladys, used to call her all the time. They were in a book club and they were both part of a group of ladies who met for lunch now and then. Gladys kept calling her for the first year, tried to get her out, came to visit, but then Martha would make excuses and Gladys finally stopped calling. Now there's just me. Martha doesn't answer the phone any more. Like I said, I don't know what to do.

I tried to get her to go to therapy, but of course that involved going out and she'd just pull inside—set her mouth and shake her head and say "No, no, I can't I wish I could. I know I should. But I can't."

I joined a group, one of those support groups for spouses and care givers of agoraphobics and they all had little hints, tricks, plans, but they also had their stories and after awhile I realized I wasn't getting anywhere. I kept going though. I kept hoping someone would have a strategy that seemed to work. I don't know.

One of the other guys in the group (they were mostly guys; it seems most agoraphobics are women), seemed like a nice guy and an interesting one too and besides he'd managed to have some limited success with his wife, getting her to go to church, for example and once in a while going with him to the coffee shop. She still wouldn't go out alone though, although he was working on it. She wasn't quite as bad as Martha. She liked gardening and she'd work in her yard, at least the back yard where she wasn't likely to meet anybody else. She also had no problem talking on the phone. In fact, she talked on the phone all the time, especially to some old friends who had moved to California. They didn't know she was agoraphobic and she told them lies about going to the theater and being in a dinner club and what all she did with her friends.

"One step at a time," Bill said. Bill was the husband's name. He was retired too, a balding guy with a comb over that was pretty ridiculous, but everything else about him was very down to earth and common sense. "Don't ask her to go to the theater or out to dinner. Just take her hand and say, 'Let's walk to the end of the sidewalk. Just the end of the sidewalk and back. I'll hold your hand the whole way.' Then after she gets OK with this, you can take a few steps beyond the sidewalk and eventually the end of the block. Not too fast. Don't push it. Be patient. One step at a time."

"Here," I said to Martha, "do something for me. When you get the mail, don't hold onto the screen door. Step out on the first step. Let the door close. Pick up the mail. Take a big breath. Then open the door and come on back in."

Martha looked as if I'd asked her to do cartwheels naked down the middle of the street.

"Oh, honey," she said, "Oh, come on. I know what you're up to. If I do that, next thing you know you'll have me taking another step down. Then another. There are four steps there. And then the sidewalk and then you'll want to go bowling and out for pizza pie. There's just no end to what you'll want me to do."

I couldn't deny it. She was right. She was absolutely right. Charlie Apple was right too. I didn't want him just to cut his weeds and take care of his property, I wanted him to lower his price to something reasonable, sell it to someone who would build a house. Maybe a young couple. A young couple with children. They'd have a swing set and a dog and I'd talk to the husband about local politics and Martha would have coffee with the wife and she'd make cookies for the kids and I'd tell the kids stories sitting on our porch swing and the kids would call me uncle and we'd be good neighbors and there would be no more hurricanes and we'd all live happily ever after.

I asked her if she was afraid of hurricanes. After all, it all really started after the storm. The agoraphobia I mean and she looked at me like I was crazy. "Aren't you?" she asked. I had to admit I was. I still went out though. How can you not go out? Besides staying in the house was no guarantee of safety. Look at Charlie Apple's house next door. Or rather look at that empty lot. The hurricane smashed that house. They were just plain dumb lucky it didn't kill them all.

That, of course, was the wrong thing to say. Next day I noticed the blinds were shut on all the windows on the side of the house facing the empty lot. Oh no, I thought. One down. Three to go. I was determined she wouldn't pull the blinds down in the rest of the house.

She liked watching me. She liked that. She liked to sit in the kitchen, something gourmet simmering on the stove, a pie in the oven, sit with a cup of coffee at the table and watch me through the window planting outside, creating for her a safe and beautiful world, green and flowering and lush and luxuriant, inviting, seductive, aromatic. "Come," it said. "Come and feel me. Smell me. Place your cheek against this fragile earth and imagine for a moment it is not spinning, not turning, but is firm and unmoving and utterly, utterly safe."

I was determined to seduce her into this world. The real world, the world where people went about their business and pleasure as if their common fate did not matter at all, scarcely didn't exist, what with all the beauty around them. Wasn't that enough? Wouldn't that do? Couldn't she, for God's sake, realize we all were in the same boat, the same, same boat, my darling. Hang on! I can hold your hand. I can't save you. I can't save anyone. Who do you think I am, anyway? What do you expect? Aren't I enough? Not enough for sure. But enough anyway? Please, please. You can be afraid, but you cannot, I won't let you give up. Look at me. See how I'm working? Watch. At least do that. Can you? Please?

On the anniversary of the storm I bought a car load of flowers. There were impatiens and lantana and daisies. There was more honeysuckle, more pansies, more of everything. More, more, more. I would fill up the garden with color, the backyard with spectacle, the world with impossible to ignore beauty.

I didn't look at the window where I knew she was watching. I dug, I turned the earth. I mixed in the fertilizer and the extra top soil. I punched the holes for seeds and dug the trenches for the plants. I placed them carefully, patted the earth. I stood and danced along the fence with my trowel and finally I looked at the window where she stood, face pressed against the glass, her eyes full of tears, her mouth open with longing and despair and as I watched she slowly lowered the blind.

No! I was full of rage, an adrenaline pumped, hot and hellacious anger. I would pull her out, push her face in the dirt, open her arms to the sky, pull her clothes off and roll her in the flowers, open her eyes to what she was doing! No! I ran to the kitchen door and pulled it open, slamming it against the side of the house. She looked up at me with fear. She knew I was completely out of control. But I knew. I knew what I wanted and I was going to get it. I grabbed her wrist, pulled her toward the door. She sat down on the floor and flailed her legs crying "No! No! Please. No."

But I wouldn't listen. I pulled her up with a strength I thought I had lost. I pulled her through the door. We stumbled on the steps and she said, "Wait, wait. My knee. Look. It's bleeding." But I wouldn't listen. I pulled her back to the fence line. I pushed her down to her knees. I pushed a trowel into her hand.

"Now dig!" I screamed. "Dig! Pull up everything. Go ahead! Destroy it! Pull it all up! You close that blind and it's all destroyed anyway. You think I care about any of this? I don't care. I don't give a shit about any of it! It's for you! It's all for you. You don't want it, then you are going to by God destroy it yourself!"

She was crying, whimpering really and when I turned away she got up and ran to the door. I ran after her. She tried to lock the door to keep me out, but I pushed the door in and she went sprawling to the floor. "Please. Please," she pleaded.

"Get up," I said.

She scooted backward and then she ran. She ran up the stairs and I let her go. I heard the door to our bedroom close and the click of the lock. I opened the blinds on the kitchen window.

My breathing slowed. I sat at the table and thought of nothing. And then I started to cook. I found her recipe for veal Marsala. I made it, following the instructions carefully. I also made chicory with fava beans and angel hair pasta.

When everything was ready I went upstairs and knocked on the bedroom door. "Dinner is ready," I said. No answer. "I've made veal Marsala. Probably not as good as yours, but still." No answer.

I went downstairs again and got my saber saw from the laundry room. I went back upstairs and sawed a rectangle out of the bottom of the door. Later, I thought, I'll get some hinges and make a little swinging door. I carefully swept up the sawdust and went back to the kitchen.

I put the meal on a plate, wrapped utensils in a cloth napkin, poured a glass of wine. Then I took the food upstairs and slid it into the bedroom. I heard the springs of the bed as she got up. I sat against the stair banister for awhile and then I went downstairs and cleaned the kitchen.

I don't work in the garden much anymore. The whole place has pretty much gone to seed. Weeds everywhere. I never much liked it anyway. I only did it for Martha. I've really gotten into the cooking though. I've even added to her recipe collection. I can see how she got addicted to the food channel. It's not just the food. You really learn a lot about culture and about people by learning what they eat.

The meals I make for her are pretty spectacular. They really are. Eggs Benedict. Homemade soups and panini. Prime rib. Shrimp and okra gumbo. Crème brulee. Foie gras and toast points. Caviar. I've even started to make homemade pasta and bread.

The master bedroom is attached to a bathroom. There's a TV and a radio in there too, so she's got everything she needs. The door is locked from the inside, not the outside so she can come out any time she wants. She's free to go which is a laugh because obviously she's not going anywhere.

After a few days I sat outside the door, my back to the banister, my legs pulled up and my chin on my knees and I talked. I was very calm. I told her I had noticed from the outside that she had hung something (it looked like an old robe) over the window. I reminded her how she used to like looking at the sunlight on the ceiling during the day and the shadows on the wall at night. Now I don't notice any light at all. I talked about our life together. I didn't pull any punches. I wasn't worried any more. I didn't try to be understanding or kind. I told her I thought she was completely crazy. I told her I loved her. She didn't say anything.

There is some evidence that when I leave the house she comes out of the room. I've noticed little things. Something small has been moved. A spoon in the sink. A magazine on the coffee table not quite where I left it. I don't mention any of this.

Every night I tell her goodnight. One night I heard a small voice and a shadow on the floor and I think a hand near the opening at the bottom of the door (I never did buy those hinges.) Then the hand was withdrawn. The small voice said, "Honey?"

"Yes?" I said as gently as I could. There was a long pause and then she said, "Do you remember our trip to New York?"

"Yes," I said, a bitterness returning because I knew there would be no more trips to anywhere.

"That was a lot of fun," she said.

We talked. We even laughed. She remembered the plays we saw, all the sights. Central Park. The Empire State Building. Greenwich Village. The nice restaurants. The shopping.

"I bought that scarf."

"Yes. The one you lost later."

"Oh, yes."

We talked for an hour without ever admitting or referring to the absurdity of our situation. The sawed through door between us. Then she said, "Good night, honey. Sweet dreams." And I said, "Sweet dreams too." I heard her move away.

The one thing I worry about is the matches. I know there is a candle in the bathroom and in the saucer beside the candle is a box of matches. I don't think it's likely she would use them, but I would be happier if they weren't there.

Hurricane season begins next week. I've noticed that the TV in the bedroom is almost permanently set to the weather channel and I don't think this is a good sign. Yesterday she told me she was worried because her room was on the top of the house and any tree that hit it would get her first. I told her there were no longer any trees near our house tall enough to fall through the roof except for the live oak in the front and that wasn't very likely to fall even in a category 5 hurricane. She begged me to have it taken down, but it's on city property as I pointed out to her and anyway I'd never do that.

"I know I'm being silly," she said.

"Yes," I said, "Yes, you are."

"Will you call the city?"

"I'll call the city," I lied, "but, I know what they'll say. They'll say they can't destroy a perfectly good tree just because some crazy lady is afraid."

"That's what I am, aren't I?"

"Yes, darling, that's what you are."

I am hopeful now. Maybe her fear of the tree falling will push her out of the room, down the stairs, into the rest of the house. Like Bill said, "Whatever works. One step at a time. Be patient."

I'm trying.

I'm trying to be patient, but more and more I worry about those matches. Martha really is crazy. Who knows what she'll do?

GEOMETRY

I remember only two things from high school geometry. One is the curve of Christine Carter's right breast, visible in front of me as she lounged to the left of her desk, and the other is the principle that two points determine a line and three points determine a plane.

At one point in my life, thirty years ago, I was living in Nice, France. I had so far successfully negotiated the Vietnam war by extending my education status into graduate school, and when that had been eliminated, by lucking out with a lottery number of 234. Now, as more and more young and even not so young men were being sent over to no discernible purpose (my view then and now), I was awaiting anxiously the magic birthday that would render my being drafted, while not impossible, at least highly unlikely.

Two points determine a line. Point one, I am an overeducated dropout on the Riviera. Point two, I am an underachieving middle manager in the old/new city of New Orleans.

It is Mardi Gras. Yesterday a majorette from St. Claude High School was raped and killed after the Orpheus parade. Her picture in the paper shows a pretty light skinned black girl with short hair, twirling a baton and high stepping in white boots and tassels.

The *Nicois* love parties. And, of course, they pride themselves on being vacationland. It's not surprising then that Mardi Gras is a big time in Nice. It's smaller in scale than New Orleans, but it's still really good. The big thing back then (maybe now too, I don't know) was confetti (accent on last syllable). You could buy a big bag of it for a *franc* and then happily toss it up, around, or even at people. Teenage boys predictably chased pretty girls and pelted their heads and backsides with huge handfuls. The girls squealed, laughed, pouted, and pretended to be angry.

The other big thing was majorettes (accent also on last syllable.) As far as I could see marching bands with genuine majorettes with short skirts, white boots and tassels were strictly an import item, unambiguously made in the USA. Several enterprising American high school bands of decidedly mediocre talent, but top heavy with perky majorettes, found their way presumably through innumerable car washes and uncounted bake sales and candy bars into the carnival parades in Nice. The crowds loved them.

That's where I saw the old drum major. That's what I called him anyway. He was red haired and freckled. His hair was thinning now and his freckles were mixed with age spots on his flaking, sunburned skin. But it was him all right. He had a wispy, transparent mustache now, but it couldn't hide the thin upper and the full lower lips that seemed to curl outward over his receding chin. When he smiled he flashed gold, which clashed with his carrot top complexion. It was him.

I hadn't seen the drum major in—what?—fifteen years? No, more like eighteen. Since I was eight or nine. Something like that. And then I only saw him the one time. Now he walked alongside the band, a probable parent, at any rate a "Band Booster" as the lettering on his green satin jacket proclaimed.

He marched by, grinning on the *Promenade des Anglais*, head high, sweat beading on his nose and chin, in step (but with studied nonchalance) with the horribly out of tune teenagers playing a brassy rendition of "When the Saints Go Marching In." The majorettes wore short pleated white skirts and when they twirled they provided flashes of green panties and an occasional untucked buttock peeping out from the shiny satin. The crowd loved them. So did I.

The same year I took geometry in high school I also took English literature. In my lit class a very fat balding teacher with a habit of plaid short sleeve shirts and chinos and brown suede shoes told us about James Joyce and epiphanies, those little moments of revelation that accent an otherwise rather ordinary existence. I was enthralled by the bird girl in the water and found nothing in my own life quite so achingly erotic as the strand of green seaweed on her milky white thigh.

I didn't actually think about the bird girl then, watching the flash of rounded flesh tucked into and out of green satin, but later in my room I wrote a poem, (I still wrote poetry then), that used that Joycean allusion to good advantage and set the bird girl twirling.

I did think of something else though.

Not the first time I saw carrot top. No, it was a couple of years earlier. I was six or seven, something like that, living in Eastlake, Ohio on a turn of road that backed into Lake Erie and whose center strip was planted with apple trees. Our house was right on the lake, or rather right on a cliff that descended some thirty feet to the lake and a thin strip of beach permanently littered with driftwood and debris. The house was cheap because every year the lake got a good three or four inches closer. True, our lifetime was secure, since the house was perhaps fifty feet from the cliff edge, but it made us feel precarious. Eventually we moved to Cleveland Heights where no such threat was evident and where the name "the Heights" had a certain cachet.

Anyway, when I was six or seven I was walking down the road (no sidewalk) from the little store where I'd buy my baseball cards, cokes and candy, and if I were feeling particularly prosperous, my Hostess cupcakes. I was sucking on a jawbreaker, a candy I didn't particularly like, but which had the virtue of longevity. The weeds were high on the side of the road and I had extracted a tall tassel from the three foot stalks and stuck it expertly in my mouth pinching out the juice and chewing happily. The insects were buzzing. (It was the middle of summer.) I don't know if you've ever walked in tall weeds over a long stretch, but if you ever have you know that the grasshoppers set up a wave pattern in front of you. They wait for you to almost get on them, then they jump—not to the side but straight forward, stupidly, for in a stride you're past them and then they sit wondering, I suppose, what that giant wanted in the neighborhood. Meantime their cousins up ahead are jumping too and their cousins a few steps behind have probably already forgotten about you. It's a continuous sensation of jumping and the clatter is loud and steady. At that moment, probably kicking at the weeds to provoke a little more noise and activity than was strictly necessary, I had a thought. It wasn't an earth shattering thought. I didn't stop in my tracks or anything like that. It was just a thought, probably like a million other thoughts people have, thoughts that come unbidden into a passive mind, a mind in this case of a six year old sucking on a jawbreaker, aware of the warmth of the sun and the clatter of the grasshoppers and not much else, barely, I suppose, considering my age, able to read, given (I admit) to musings and daydreaming, but not much to sustained thought about anything too heavy—and there it was: a thought. What I thought just then in the middle of the summer, jawbreaker creating abundant sweet saliva, sneakered feet creating panic among the grasshoppers, was this: "Before you know it, it will be Christmas."

Now by itself this thought is not so startling. I suppose every little kid has had it. Certainly every adult has. The thought, that is, that time sure does go fast. Or, perhaps more philosophically, that time is a relative thing after all and tends to stretch and snap, rush and dawdle as the occasion demands. But I didn't stop with that simple thought. Epiphany! I amended this first thought with a second, which was, after all, merely an extension, simple and obvious as all great thoughts are, namely: "When Christmas does come I'll remember this moment."

And sure enough, a half year later in my flannel pjs and wooly slippers, sitting amidst the wrapping paper, sucking on a pre-breakfast candy cane and trying to decide whether to put together my P-38 model or to go outside and try my new Flexible Flyer, I remembered. It scared the hell out of me. I suppose six year olds have had more dramatic introductions to mortality, but this one was mine and it was quite enough, thank you.

I have forgotten any more of the particulars of that Christmas day. It doesn't rank in my memory like the year (sixth grade) I had an infected ingrown toenail and had to sit with my leg raised, my big toe daubed with a foul smelling goo and throbbing with sharp pain at every heartbeat. But every few months, apropos of nothing, my mouth will fill with the taste of jawbreaker and even leaning over the frozen foods in the A&P my back will be warmed with a summer sun and my ears filled with the clack of grasshoppers. Mortality again. Time. God, could it be twenty years ago? Thirty? Forty? Soon to be more?

It was the drum major I was talking about. Of course he wasn't a drum major now—then....Now—then—in the sixties when I lived in Nice the drum major was not a drum major but a parent in booster club jacket and I was in my late twenties living in the Hotel Letitia and worrying about Vietnam.

OK. I fought my way along the crowd of confetti throwing *Nicois* on the *Promenade des Anglais* and skirting the Negresco and the Casino came out at the park where I knew the parade disbanded. I wanted to watch the drum major in action, try to see which kid was his. I don't know. I wanted to see the end of the story.

He seemed to pay more attention to a cute blonde flute player than anyone else and I heard her say, "I'll see you on the beach, Daddy, in plenty of time. We're going to get something to eat." He hugged her and then walked down the Rue Victor Hugo and back to the Promenade toward an expensive outdoor café I wouldn't be caught dead in since it was both overpriced and also entirely filled with Germans, British, and Americans, not a Frenchman in sight except the waiters. I lounged about and watched him drink an inappropriate glass of red wine, looking first satisfied and then bored, and after he paid, I followed him again.

The sun was setting and there was promise of fireworks in the Old Town later. I had meant to go down to the beach for a look after dinner, but I decided to follow the drum major instead. He retraced his steps along the Rue Victor Hugo and turned down the Rue de France. I knew that the Rue de France, just two streets back from the Promenade was where the whores worked, but it was pretty early and besides I didn't know if he knew. After three blocks of walking he turned into a small street and returned to the beach. We watched the fireworks together, unbeknownst to him. Halfway through he was joined by his daughter and a half dozen other kids from the band. I was hungry but I wanted to see what he would do next. When the last burst died away over the old fort east of the Promenade he told the kids to go on back to the hotel and then he turned again toward the

Rue de France. This time they were out in force. Hot pants, miniskirts, little fur jackets, tall leather boots. They were unmistakable in their profession. Three stood on the corner across from Frank's Bar and Grill. I swear to you, that's the name of the place: Frank's Bar and Grill. It had pictures of the Grand Canyon and the New York skyline next to the jukebox.

He approached one of the girls and the other two moved away politely. I pretended to be looking in the window of an Algerian bakery. His French was horrible.

"*Qu'est-ce-que c'est le prix?*"

"*Soixante dix-huit francs.*"

Seventy-eight francs? Why such an odd number I wondered. Why not eighty or seventy-five or a hundred? I looked at her. She was beautiful. Striking even. Over six foot tall in her white high heeled boots. Her copper orange fox jacket matched the thin red hair of my drum major. Her own hair was deep black and fell straight and long down her back. I fancied I could smell her perfume until I realized one of the other girls had approached me. She was a small, thin Vietnamese girl and she smiled boldly and asked, "*Voulez-vous venir avec moi?*"

Stupidly I stared. I had never used a prostitute. Used. Yes, that was the word. Crazily I felt jealous of the drum major who had chosen the tall beautiful one. But then....

"*Qu-est-ce que c'est le prix?*"

"*Cent francs.*"

"*Pas soixante dix-huit?*"

"*Soixante dix-huit? Non. Cent francs.*"

"*Vous avez une chambre?*"

"*Oui. Tout pret.*"

I was eight or nine when I followed the drum major down the dusty road. The drum major had appeared like a vision at the Conoco station, hatless but otherwise got up in green flannel jacket and gold epaulets, shiny silver buttons, cape with high collar, white gloves, gold stripe along the seam of his pants, golden sash and white buck shoes.

His car had broken down and he needed a ride to a parade somewhere. Where was the parade in the middle of summer? Maybe it was a band camp or something. Looking back I realize he was a high school boy, but then he seemed huge and imposing in his uniform although his weak chin and his light complexion made him seem incongruous in all that finery.

There were several boys with me at the Conoco station, drinking cokes and watching Ed fix Loren's bike. Ed was the only adult at the station and there were no customers except us kids so no one could give him a ride. Ed thought about it a lot and the drum major worried about being late and finally Ed offered to call the sheriff. "Or if you want," he said, "you can hike another half mile to the Shell. They have towing, so someone's bound to be free to drive you. How far you got to go?" And that's what he decided. The drum major set off down the road toward the Shell station and all the kids, five or six of us, set off behind him pretending to be a band.

At first he smiled at us in a friendly, nervous way and then he tried to ignore us, but we set up a steady vocal drum beat and the spirited singing of "Be Kind to Your Web Foot-ed Friends" forced his feet into a march and on we strutted down the road, drum major in front with red face and sweat pouring off his forehead and half a dozen kids stomping enthusiastically in the dust which rose and fell settling in a thin glaze on the drum major's white buck shoes. We finally got tired and turned back to the Conoco, leaving the drum major to march on in search of rescue, trying to get to his parade.

I never saw him again until that day on the *Promenade des Anglais*. Somewhere in between he had a life. I suppose I did too, but walking into the room above Frank's Bar and Grill with the girl named Nhu it seemed to me that time had snapped together again and I would remember when Easter rose, this carnival, this moment, and so it happened, and so too now on a distant Ash Wednesday I stare at the picture in the *Times-Picayune* of another majorette, another Mardi Gras, and I hear the clicking rustle of waves of grasshoppers, I taste the sweet jawbreaker, I see sweet flaky Algerian pastries through the dusty front window clouded with my own breath,

I smell the sweat and the perfume of the Rue de France. The drum major, if he's still alive, is now an old man. His pretty daughter has probably abandoned the flute. She is probably married, has kids of her own. The drum major is a grandpa. The smiling face of a now dead majorette looks out at me from the newspaper. Two points determine a line. Three points determine a plane. But there are so many points. How to choose? I can't possibly remember them all.

DEATH OF A TORTOISE

Scene One: The Tortoise Circumnavigates the Room

When Robert Sanders tried to open his kitchen door to get into his house, the door only opened a foot or so before encountering an obstruction. Robert didn't need to peek through the opening to see what the obstruction was, but he did so anyway and confirmed what he already knew. His tortoise, Buddy, big as a turkey platter, had decided to nap in front of the door.

"Buddy," Robert said, "move it, Buddy. Out of the way, big boy." He bumped the tortoise with the door and after a moment the head appeared and then the legs and the tortoise phlegmatically waddled off away from the banging door. Robert entered his house, opened the refrigerator and grabbed lettuce, carrots and grapes.

"You hungry, Buddy?"

He placed the food in the tin pie plate on the floor. He lifted up the unprotesting tortoise and looked into his placid face. "I got lettuce, Buddy. I got carrots. I got grapes. You are one lucky tortoise." Then he set the tortoise on the floor by the plate.

After fixing himself a cup of darjeeling tea, Robert sat at his dining room table which was covered with woodworking tools and meticulous quarter inch scale drawings on graph paper. He was building from scratch an exact model of the B-24 Flying Fortress. The B-24 was his thirty-seventh model in his long range project of making models of all the planes used in World War II.

As Robert worked on his model, his tortoise Buddy walked slowly through the dining room into the living room and began his accustomed circumnavigation of the walls. He walked steadily and with no apparent destination in mind and when he encountered a wall he seemed surprised and then turned left and continued on his plodding way keeping his right legs closer to the base boards. Upon encountering a corner and another wall, he would again react with seeming surprise as if this had not happened a thousand times before, and after a moment's hesitation he would lumber about and eventually negotiate a left turn before continuing on his way until once again he would encounter a wall. In this way he continued around and around the room.

Scene Two: The Hospice Patient

Robert missed the house the first time he drove by and missed it again on his way back. He had to pull into another driveway and turn around. "Third time's a charm," he said to himself. "Privet. Bamboo. Number on the mailbox. There it is."

He pulled into a dusty shell driveway and parked next to a red rusty pickup. He took off his sunglasses, pinned his name tag to his shirt and got out. A skinny black dog with mange walked up to him wagging his tail. Robert offered his hand which the dog first sniffed and then licked. Robert knocked on the aluminum screen door of the old paint peeling shotgun and a moment later the venetian blind parted and a face looked out. The door opened to reveal a big bosomed elderly lady with incongruous bleached blond hair and a dirty t-shirt. She was smoking a cigarette despite the sign on the door warning "No Smoking. Oxygen in Use."

"Hi," Robert said, "I'm Robert Sanders. I'm a hospice volunteer. I believe Gordon told you I was coming."

The woman was probably younger than Robert's sixty years but she looked older. "You with the hospice?" she asked.

"Yes. Did Gordon tell you I was coming?"

"Come on in."

"Thanks."

The front room was dominated by a huge TV which at the moment was showing two black women screaming at each other with a studio audience cheering them on. An over-weight young woman in cut off jeans was sitting at a computer. A young man was asleep on the couch covered with a dirty throw in garish orange and pink plaid.

"I'm Mary," the woman said, "he's back there." She indicated the only way he could go in the shotgun house, through an arch where Robert could see a hospital bed and a jumble of boxes labeled "adult diapers" and "protein drinks." The man in the bed seemed impossibly thin. His eyes were closed. When Robert walked into the bedroom the man opened his eyes and put out his hand.

"Hi, I'm Robert from the hospice. You up for a little visit?" He took the man's hand and was surprised when he didn't let go. The sounds of screaming and bleeped out cursing from the TV were reaching a crescendo. The audience was chanting.

"I'm Buddy," the man said. "I got me the cancer." Finally he let go of Robert's hand. "Sit down."

Robert looked around for a place to sit. There was only one chair and it was covered with half folded laundry and boxes of fruit punch and pudding. He cleaned off the chair and sat down.

From the living room, the yelling from the TV was now being echoed by Mary and the overweight girl. "I have not, Mama! I only been on the computer for half an hour. You know I'm fixing to go to work. You taking me?"

"Don't I always?"

"No. Sometimes Kyle takes me."

"Well, Kyle isn't taking you today. Kyle is asleep."

"I know that!"

Buddy began banging on the bed frame with an old bent spoon. "Mary! Mary!"

Mary appeared, "What you want, baby? You need your methadone?"

"No. I want a cigarette."

Robert didn't like to see Buddy smoking, even though he could see the oxygen unit next to the bed and knew it was safely turned off. He noticed several burn marks on the old comforter on the bed and a thin covering of ash on the floor. Mary handed Buddy a cigarette and lit it with a lighter she pulled out of her shorts.

"What's Darlene yelling about?"

"Oh, nothing. Same old, same old."

"Well, tell her to pipe down!"

"OK. OK." Voices in the next room were raised again. Apparently Kyle was up and arguing with his sister. "Oh Lord, it's always something." Mary went back in the living room to restore order.

Buddy looked at Robert and shook his head. "You got kids?" he asked.

"Yes. Two. A boy and a girl."

"Grandkids?"

"Four. They live in Florida."

"I got me four."

"Grandkids?"

"No. Kids. Two grandkids. There's their pictures over there."

Robert looked at the wall and saw a boy in a little league uniform and a girl in a tutu smiling out of ceramic frames with "I ♥ Grandpa" on the bottom. Robert felt a surge of guilt for thinking Buddy's family was so much different from his own. Those two could be his own grandkids. He even had pictures in those very same frames.

Buddy let out a grunt and raised himself off the bed with his skinny arms. His cigarette fell and rolled onto the floor. Robert picked it up. Buddy lowered himself with an exhalation of breath and then banged with his spoon on the bed frame. Mary appeared immediately.

"You OK, baby?"

"I believe I need my methadone."

"OK, baby." She disappeared into the kitchen.

"You OK?" Robert asked.

"It'll pass."

Mary returned with a needleless syringe filled with a pink liquid. Buddy stuck the syringe into his mouth and pushed the plunger. Mary took the syringe from him and Buddy lay back on his pillow.

"You want your oxygen, baby?"

"I believe I better."

"No smoking now."

"I know that. You too, unless you go outside."

"I know." Carefully Mary placed the oxygen hose into his nose, wrapped it around his ears and loosened it in the front. Then she turned on the unit. It began to bubble and hum. Buddy closed his eyes. Robert's visit was over.

Scene Three: The woman in the coffee shop

On the way home from his hospice visit Robert decided to stop at PJ's for a coffee. As he drove into the parking lot he wondered if he should tell Buddy that he had a tortoise named Buddy too. He wondered if he'd be insulted. Probably not. Get a kick out of it? Probably.

At the counter of the shop he ordered his usual, not any of the fancy drinks, but a simple small dark roast black. After paying he looked around for a place to sit and saw a woman who looked familiar. Oh, yes. She was a member of the old dinner club that he and his wife Janet used to belong to before Janet died. He hadn't seen the woman since Janet's funeral. Ten years. What was her name? He couldn't recall. He used to be good at names. Now they eluded him. He used to be good at Jeopardy too. He would keep score as he watched and usually did as well or better than the contestants. Now he recognized what or who the answer was, could see or hear it on the periphery of his brain, but more often than not it wouldn't come until the answer was given and he'd say, "Yes. I knew that." What was her name? He had heard her husband had died a few years back, very sudden. Heart attack?

She was sitting in front of a laptop computer surrounded by a pile of books and another pile of papers. She was drinking something tall and tan. A latte? Some flavored concoction? He walked up to the table.

"Hi."

The woman looked up. Her face broke into a smile. "Robert!" She surprised him by getting up and giving him a big hug. "It's been so long. How have you been?

They talked for over an hour. "Catching up" is what they called it. She told him she had gone back to school and got a degree in kinesiology. She was teaching p.e. in a middle school. He told her about his hospice work and his model building hobby. She did not tell him about her daughter's current messy divorce. He did not tell her that since his wife's death he had slowly and unconsciously fallen into a very isolated and lonely life. He and Janet had had a perfect marriage and now, after most of their friends (they had been Janet's friends really) had drifted away he was left to himself. He did not tell her he couldn't for the life of him remember her name.

Midway through the conversation she said, "We should get together. Have dinner or something." What he should have said, of course, was something like, "Great idea. How about this Friday? We could go to Middendorf's." What he did say was, "Absolutely. Let's do that." He thought perhaps he saw a small flicker of disappointment but he couldn't be sure and he left it at that.

After awhile she looked at her watch and announced, "Oh dear, I'm going to be late," and began picking up her things. Then she added "I was serious about getting together." Once again, however, Robert only said, "Yes. I would love that." And then he pulled out a card from his wallet and handed it to her. "Here's my phone number and email. Give me a call. We'll make some plans." He hoped that she would give him a card too, one with her name on it, but she only took the card and put it in her purse.

Robert hoped she would give him another hug and he wasn't disappointed, but as she left the shop her name was still maddeningly absent from his memory and he knew that the next days (he hoped not weeks) he would obsessively wait for her to call him.

Scene Four: Death of a Tortoise

In the next ten days Robert visited Buddy and his family three times. Each visit was much the same. The same battling siblings, the same execrable TV program, the oxygen, the methadone, the thin figure in the bed for brief moments talking about sports or religion or grandchildren, increasingly falling asleep with the oxygen unit humming in the background.

Each day Robert waited for a phone call from the woman. He compulsively checked his email. He told himself, "I'm being a fool. She probably has no real desire to see me. And it's not as if she's such a great beauty or anything." Still, he tried over and over to try to remember her name.

On the tenth day he awoke to find that his tortoise had died. There had been no sign, no warning. He had no idea how old the tortoise was. He had been full grown when he bought him. And the day before had been exactly the same as any other day. Buddy ate and slept and walked endlessly around the living room keeping the wall to his right, negotiating each left turn with elaborate awkward care. Now he was dead.

A tortoise does not offer much in the way of affection. Still, now that he was dead, Robert knew he would miss him. He picked him up and held the big guy against his chest. Robert realized with surprise that he was crying. The phone rang. For the first time in ten days his heart did not leap at the sound of the phone. He answered it. "Hi, Robert. This is Gordon. I'm calling to tell you that Buddy has died."

At first Robert was confused. And then he realized that Gordon wasn't talking about his tortoise but about his hospice patient. He carefully wrote down all the information. Wake. Funeral. Time and place.

When he hung up he placed the tortoise on the floor and went in search of his gardening gloves. He remembered back almost nine years ago. It was after Janet died. He had had Buddy for almost two years and if truth be told, Robert was growing tired of seeing him walk obsessively and perhaps neurotically around and around the living room. He wondered if perhaps Buddy longed for his freedom. Or at the very least the feel of real ground beneath his feet. Grass. Dirt.

He wondered about maybe taking him out in the country and letting him go, but decided against it. Perhaps Buddy had lost his ability to take care of himself. He compromised and took him outside and set him down in the middle of the back yard. He would be free to stay or free to go. It was Buddy's choice. Every day for a week, Robert checked on him and every day Buddy was in a different place, but he never left the yard. He brought him back into the house and the tortoise began to walk around the living room wall.

Now as he put on his gardening gloves, picked up his shovel and began to dig a grave, he wondered if the other Buddy had ever had a chance to escape. Well, of course, he had a chance. He could have gone, left. Did he recognize his chance and let it pass? Did he have any regrets? He carried the tortoise to the side of his garden and buried him next to the wooden fence.

Scene Five: A Phone Call

One evening, two weeks after his tortoise died, Robert was seated at his dining room table working on a quarter inch scale drawing of the tail assembly of the B-24 Flying Fortress, when the phone rang. He looked at the caller i.d. which said "Colleen Landry." He didn't know any Colleen Landry but he answered the phone and said "Hello."

"Hello. Robert?" It was her, the woman in the coffee shop.

"Colleen?"

"No, Colleen is my sister. This is Roberta."

Roberta. Yes, of course. That was her name. Only one letter different from his own. And then in a flash he remembered her last name too. Smith. Roberta Smith. How could he have forgotten such a simple name?

"Oh. Roberta. I didn't recognize you. Good to hear from you. How have you been?"

"Oh, I'm fine. Listen, Robert, I have a big favor to ask you."

"Sure thing. What do you need?"

"It's about my father. He's moved in with my sister and he's becoming somewhat of a problem. For one thing he's very sick. Long list. Diabetes. Emphysema. He has a wound on his foot that won't heal. High blood pressure. He's very overweight. And to tell you the truth he can be something of a pill. He's driving my sister crazy."

"Mm-hmm." Robert's eyes strayed back to his scale drawing of the bomber's tail section.

"I remembered you told me that you visited hospice patients. My dad isn't in hospice, but the thing is Colleen has this dentist appointment on Monday and I have to work and well, I was wondering—I know it's a big favor—but would you be willing to come and visit, stay with him for a couple of hours while she went to the dentist?"

Robert reminded her that if he did come and visit it would be a strictly personal thing. He would not be doing it as a representative of the hospice and Roberta assured him she understood. Robert knew that he was being asked to do something ordinarily left to either best friends or professionals, but he also knew that he was going to say yes. He wondered if saying yes made it less or more likely she would agree to go out with him. "Go out," he thought, "what an odd expression." It would be dinner. A date. That's what it was really. Robert had not been on a date in decades. Would she say yes only because she felt obligated? Would she resent him? Or worse, feel pity? He told her yes, of course, he'd be glad to help.

Roberta was relieved and very grateful. She thanked him over and over. "You always were such a nice man."

Robert deflected this praise and asked for the particulars. Time. Place. Then he said, "What's your phone number?"

"You can reach Colleen at…."

"No. No. I mean your number."

Robert detected a tiny hesitation, but then she gave him her number and he wrote it down on the edge of his scale model drawing and read it back to her to make sure he got it right. He even said, "We really do have to get together for dinner" and after another tiny hesitation Roberta agreed. They talked a little while more, then they hung up.

Robert rewrote the phone number on a piece of paper, folded it in half and put it in his wallet. He would call her, but not right away. He would wait, make her wait as he had waited. Two weeks maybe. By then he would have visited her dad, met her sister. They would have things to talk about. Robert realized as he made these plans that what he was feeling most of all, what was rising in him like the mercury in a thermometer was a hot and horrible flush of excruciating anger. He allowed himself to feel it, identify it for what it was, let it run its course, and then he walked outside into the darkness of his backyard. He stood by the disturbed soil at the edge of his garden where he had buried his tortoise, looked up into the night sky and wept because he knew the list of regrets in his life was growing, ever growing and there was no end in sight except the end that he shared with absolutely everyone else in the world: the pilots and crews of those World War II planes, his hospice patients, Roberta's dad, his lost tortoise, everyone and everything and this made him not so much sad as relieved, at least relieved enough to return to his desk and finish his quarter inch scale drawing. It was very late when he finished.

St. Vincent De Paul

Elise had read the email from her grandson and then she had slept on it, putting off a decision. When she awoke in the morning the email was the first thing on her mind, but she quickly put it away and instead carefully undid the long gray braid of her hair that hung nearly to her waist and stepped into the shower. She washed her thick hair carefully and put in conditioner and then toweled and air dried and brushed it over and over and let it hang free. She made a pot of oatmeal and ate it with honey and raisins and then she braided her hair again and tied a navy blue ribbon around it close to her head and sat at her desk with a second cup of coffee and put on her glasses and pulled up the email once again and read it again and then printed it, read it yet again from the paper as if it might have changed in the transfer and filed it away in her grandson's file which dated back to his childhood and contained not only emails but letters and childish drawings and birthday cards and one yellow page that chronicled over the years the checks she had sent him, the amount, the date, the response (usually blank), when they were paid back—which was never—and a running total which by now had topped twelve thousand dollars. She sat fingering the keys, composing in her head the response she would make to his latest disaster.

Elise's grandson Eric was twenty-eight years old. He lived a thousand miles away in the college town where he had gone ten years before as a freshman. For seven years he was a student, flunking out twice before finally abandoning school altogether and getting by with a series of jobs that were many and various but neatly divided into two categories: dead end slightly above minimum wage or wild and ambitious schemes sure to make him rich which never really panned out, always someone else's fault. Both categories of jobs had one thing in common—they never lasted more than a couple of months before he'd either leave for something better or just because he got bored or else he'd go and do something stupid and get himself fired.

In those ten years he had gone through six or seven cars, several of them totaled in accidents (always, he claimed, someone else's fault), maybe a dozen apartments, houses, condos, always shared, always ending badly, and too many to count girl friends, some of whom came with the living arrangements.

Eric was a charming and very nice guy who at first meeting seemed to be down to earth and straight forward, but upon closer and more extended acquaintance proved to be absolutely unreliable in every way. Elise loved him in the reflexive way of grandparents, but she had to admit that she did not like him much, hadn't liked him since maybe fifth grade, and she didn't trust anything he said or did. She knew she would die for him, but she wasn't at all sure it was a good idea to yet again advance him some dough.

It was the same old song, new verse. Broke up with Sandra (Elise had no idea who Sandra was, had never heard of Sandra), had no place to live, was crashing with Joey and Tom (two other people she had never heard of), they were getting antsy for him to leave, had a real good chance of getting this really cool apartment but needed a first and last month rent and deposit, was almost completely sure he had a job offer coming from this computer company (a real opportunity!), and he also had a broken water pump on his car and he needed a new battery to boot, and if he got the job he would need....

Elise sighed, fingered the keys, pondered her response, knew the drill, knew that half of what he said was probably bullshit, not exactly a lie just a convenient retelling of the bare facts. She didn't doubt the breakup with this Sandra or the loss of living quarters. She didn't even doubt the car problems. The job was probably not a complete fabrication, but the particulars were probably not as rosy as he had painted them.

The phone rang. It was Father Leo from church.

"I have a lady here," he said.

"Yes?"

"I tried to get ahold of Anthony, but he doesn't answer."

"That's OK, Father. I'm on duty today."

"Oh, OK."

Elise sighed. The Society of St. Vincent de Paul had a schedule of who was on duty and it was not only on their website but each week a printed copy was left with Wanda at the rectory. It was very simple. Any requests for assistance or people showing up on the church doorstep should be referred to whoever was on duty that day. Despite this, however, the priests at St. Michael's never remembered this. They only thought—"Oh, St. Vincent de Paul. This is for them" and then they'd call Anthony. And if they couldn't get Anthony, they'd call Elise.

"Who is she? What does she need?"

"Can you come down here?"

Elise sighed again. St. Michaels's was only five minutes away and it would be easier just to go than to get Father Leo to ask the woman the right questions.

"OK. I'll be right down."

Elise felt relieved that she could put off deciding what to do about her grandson's latest request, but she also felt the vague pressure of a kind of depression and anger pushing up through her chest. I shouldn't be doing this, she thought to herself for the thousandth time. I am exactly the wrong person for this job.

Ten years before, Elise had been a completely happy middle aged housewife, who loved her husband, her three grown children, five grandchildren and her life, which consisted mostly of part time work at a garden center and puttering around the house. Then her husband went out in the backyard to pick tomatoes and had a heart attack and fell over in the garden. Inside the kitchen Elise was boiling pasta and stirring sauce, slicing melons and assembling a salad, singing along to an oldies radio station with the Platters' "Only You." When it occurred to her to see what was taking her husband so long, he was dead. She wondered then and still wonders now if she had only checked earlier.... The doctors told her no, but still....

After her husband died she had time on her hands and a need to do something. She was left well off as far as money went, but the days seemed empty as did the house and her mind was empty too, refusing to think deeply about anything for fear of what might surface. She got busy, mostly at church. She worked at the local Food Pantry. She became a pink lady at the hospital. She worked first at the St. Vincent de Paul thrift store and then she joined the Society and became one of the volunteers who directly helped people with things like emergency food and lodging, help to travelers passing through, help with utility bills, furniture, clothes and groceries, whatever was needed.

When she first began working for the Society she was surprised at their rules. They seemed so arbitrary, so…well, suspicious…but then as the months and years passed she realized that there were a lot of people out there playing the system, going from one group to another, getting something here, something there, never actually making any progress, not getting back on their feet because they had never in their lives been on their feet. They lived day to day, week to week, begging in an official way, just getting by, and no thought to tomorrow. Just like her grandson, she thought bitterly, although she doubted he had ever used the services of St. Vincent de Paul.

So who would this lady be and what was her story and how plausible would it sound? Elise had heard everything. When she pulled the car up in front of the rectory she saw a plump middle aged black woman sitting in the glider on the porch. Next to her in the glider was Father Leo. They were drinking glasses of iced water. Elise pulled her book sack from the trunk. In it were all the forms and vouchers she would need. But first, the lady's story.

Father Leo introduced them and then made his escape, obviously grateful to be gone. Most people seeking help, Elise had discovered, were torn between resentment and anger for being in this inferior position and a kind of abject gratefulness that someone might want to give them something. When Elise first started doing this work she was angered at the people who seemed surly and demanding and was happy for the fawning and groveling and gratitude. But as the years went by she recognized that the more polite and ingratiating the person was, the more likely the story was bogus. On the other hand, sometimes a person in need must be really far gone to lose all desire for dignity and only the con men didn't care what you thought of them as long as they got something.

What amazed Elise was the almost infinite variety of bad things that can happen to a person and how unfairly these bad things seem to be distributed. No one just lost a job. He lost a job just at the time his mother dies or his daughter gets pregnant or his wife discovers a lump in her breast. No one just gets sick or has an accident or a run in with the law. They always seem to come in droves. So the mother of the Down syndrome girl gets diabetes, is thrown out of her apartment and then totals the car they've been living in for two weeks until their cousin can help them out with a job in Orlando if they can get there, but of course now they can't because the car is gone. And the daughter now has a urinary tract infection and the state is threatening to take her away. Things like that. Nothing is ever simple.

Elise listened to the woman's story. There were complications and a few sidebar issues Elise could do nothing about, but the essence of the story was refreshingly straightforward. Delinea (that was the woman's name) was on her way to the Gulf Coast. Her car broke down. She had no money to fix it and no money for bus fare. Her husband was on the coast roofing houses. His boss had taken off and disappeared owing him $590. The husband was now in a shelter. She herself was now traveling to meet him. She was stuck with four boxes of stuff—"everything I own"—a nonfunctioning car and $23 in cash. She was at the K-Bar Inn where she owed two nights rent. What she needed was to pay off the hotel, a bus ticket to the coast and if possible some food for the next couple of days. Her last meal had been a McMuffin the day before. She kept repeating how this was all so unfamiliar to her. "Two years ago I had a good job. I was working at a car dealership. I had a good job. My husband had a good job too. This is so terrible. I just need a little help. That's all. When I get back on my feet I'll give it all back to the St. Vincents, I can promise you that. I believe in helping people. I always have."

Elise felt little alarm bells of doubt, but she maintained a cheerful and helpful exterior and told the woman that she would drive her back to the hotel, give the hotel a voucher for the two nights she'd already been there and for one more night. Then she'd go check on bus tickets and pick up some food for her at the grocery. The woman was humbly grateful and kept assuring Elise that in the not so distant future, "The St. Vincents" would receive a generous donation from the once again independent Delinea.

In the grocery store, Elise found herself in the familiar dilemma of trying to buy appropriate food for someone who is destitute. First of all there was a fifty dollar voucher limit. Then there was the problem of selecting only ready to eat food. Then there was the more or less moral dilemma of avoiding obvious fancy and expensive foods as inappropriate and at the same time not choosing only the bad quality stuff that said "poor people food." So no smoked oysters, but no Vienna sausage or potted meat either. She didn't buy artisan bread but she didn't buy the air filled white stuff that was so cheap. She stocked up on fresh fruit, whole wheat bread, sliced ham and cheese and salami, orange juice, yogurt, granola bars, crackers and some cookies. She also bought some fried chicken and cole slaw from the deli and a liter of coke. It was a little over fifty dollars and she used her own money for the difference .

In the car, she tried getting Anthony on her cell phone but there was no answer. It was always best to check with him just to make sure that Delinea wasn't known to him already as an abuser of the system. Without his confirmation, however, she was free to use her judgment and that's what she did. Delinea was at the hotel and that was a good sign. If she were a local making up stories, she wouldn't go to that kind of trouble. Also, she had a Texas driver's license. So all in all her story was probably more or less true. Elise had no illusions that Delinea any time soon would be writing a check to "the St. Vincents", but she was nonetheless someone who clearly needed some food, some shelter and a bus ticket which would thankfully send her on her way and out of the circle of Elise's responsibility.

Delinea was watching soaps when Elise arrived and she expressed wonder and gratitude at the cornucopia of food. She was a bit miffed that the bus for the Gulf Coast left at 6 am but recovered and asked where the bus station was and how long it would take to walk there and hinted broadly that a ride would be welcome, but Elise pretended not to understand and she gave exact directions on how to walk. More profuse thanks and Elise made her escape as Delinea settled in with the fried chicken and the soaps.

When Elise entered her house, dreading the task with her grandson's email, the phone was ringing. It was Anthony, who told her they had another one, this a young man from New Orleans, who had been doing roofing. He had a pregnant girl friend, a Katrina ruined house he had escaped in Chalmette, a job offer in Pascagoula, yet another broken down car, but one that was being fixed. He was presently at the Willow courts and he and the pregnant girl friend had not eaten in two days.

Elise told Anthony about Delinea and he said he would check on her. Elise was not exactly eager to go and meet this young man and listen to yet another tale of woe, but on the other hand she didn't look forward to dealing with her grandson either, so she made a quick phone call to the Willow Courts to make sure they were there and set her alarm and went out of the house again.

When she knocked on the door she could hear the sounds of the TV inside, the droning of car engines and the excited high pitch announcer of a NASCAR race. The door opened a crack and a young, red-faced man peeked out. He had a long narrow head with prematurely thinning hair ending in a small ponytail. There was a scraggly brown beard and a no doubt fake diamond stud in his left ear.

"Hi. I'm Elise from St. Vincent."

"Oh yeah. Come on in." Immediately the look of fear and suspicion that had made his face tight opened up and he smiled, throwing the door wide. "Norma, turn down that TV."

Norma might have been a pretty girl if she had lost about fifty pounds. It wasn't just that she was pregnant, but also fat lingered in her arms, thighs and face. She wore a pair of cutoff overalls and a pink t-shirt advertising a bar in Cancun. On her right shoulder she had a tattoo of a cross.

Now that Elise stepped inside the room she began having her doubts. The first thing that made her pause was the profusion of empty fast food cartons and sacks. There was a pizzas box, a fried chicken box, a bag from McDonald's, several cups and a sack labeled Krispy-Kreme Donuts. Hadn't she been told they hadn't eaten in two days?

Elise admitted to her prejudices. She didn't like tattoos. And even though they had become much more socially acceptable (even a couple of her friends had a few discreet and tasteful ones), she retained her old feeling from her youth that only sailors and gangsters and sluts got themselves tattooed. And now that she was able to have a better look, she realized that the young man's left arm was completely tattooed as well as his shoulder which was bare due to the fact that he was wearing what they used to call a "wife beater" t-shirt. And the girl! It wasn't just a cross on her shoulder. Elise now saw down her ample cleavage that there was both a bouquet of flowers and some reptilian creature tattooed on her chest. Swirls and crescents and stars also adorned her right calf and could it be?—yes, there was a yin/yang symbol on her neck.

Food. Tattoos. But there was more. Why in the world would they be in possession of a police billy club, which was lying out on the bed? She also noted on the bedside table at least a half dozen prescription bottles. Sitting in the suitcase was a full carton of Vantage cigarettes and before the young man discreetly closed its cover, she thought she saw a plastic bag which just possibly could contain—well, of course she didn't see, but there beside the ashtray she could see a pack of cigarette papers. And what was it that the girl had hidden under her rather ample thigh when the man had opened the door and Elise had walked in?

Elise did not feel any fear. What she felt was embarrassment. She was going to have to confirm that these people deserved the aid of the St. Vincent de Paul Society and she was beginning to have her doubts.

For one thing they were white. Elise struggled with this. She was an educated and intelligent person and held no obvious racial prejudices. Over the years she had had several black friends. She had always been active in civil rights organizations and causes. She was even acutely and painfully aware of the kind of supercilious and removed liberalism that masquerades as enlightenment and was wary of becoming such a cliché herself. Despite all her best efforts, however, it never really surprised her much when a black person told her some tale of woe. A percentage of them were the cons—well, you can expect that. Most were true enough and the long list of social, familial, medical and financial disasters that afflicted so many were easily understood in the sociological context of their lives. But it always made her suspicious when a white person was similarly afflicted. Can't you get a job? She'd think. At the very least, don't you have a family? A credit card? A long, lifetime habit of being prepared rather than just living on the edge? Can't you get on? Where's your mama?

So that was always her first question—what about family?

Well, the young man, it seems did have a mama and a sister in Michigan. They were in no position to help—no details given. The young woman laughed at the possibility of getting help from her family which included a sexually abusive stepfather and an alcoholic mother. Her brother was in jail.

The young man began telling his story. Elise had learned from long experience that it was best to just keep quiet and let them talk. It was rarely possible to follow all the ins and outs and details. There was almost always something disturbing, not quite right, something missing in the narrative—and usually the something missing was the nub of the problem—but pushing for answers too early would shut them up and confused things. So let them talk.

He did. Talk. He went on for almost fifteen minutes. He described in loving detail the house he owned in Chalmette, the furniture, the big screen TV, the stereo, his car, his motorcycle—all gone in the hurricane—eight feet of flooding and a water oak and two pines through the roof. Three years ago he had been a commercial diver, real good job, security, a future, owned his own house, engaged to get married. Then came the motorcycle accident, couldn't dive anymore, a series of other jobs, medical complications (he showed her the scars on his legs and abdomen), the breakup with his fiancée, meeting Norma, finally getting himself together, a new job—and then came Katrina and the storm blew away his house, his car, his job, his whole life. He had moved up here and FEMA had been paying his way in hotels and he had been trying to find work and then Norma got pregnant and now FEMA was cutting him off and he heard about construction work in Mississippi and he was on his way when the old car he'd bought from a friend broke down and here they were and he was just about out of his pain prescriptions (his leg still bothered him a lot) and of course Norma being pregnant needed to take care of herself and if he could only get to Mississippi he was sure he could start over and be all right.

Elise asked to see his driver's license. Another alarm bell went off when the i.d. presented was not a driver's license but a state i.d. If he had a car, then why not a driver's license? She said nothing, made small talk, asked about the companies he had worked for as a diver. His answers were quick and straight forward, each one adding a few unnecessary details. "Nicest boss I ever had." "We used to be two weeks on, two weeks off. I liked that."

There were more details. It turns out Norma had had a FEMA trailer. Or rather her cousin had one and she stayed there until she kicked her out. Long story of her cousin and her husband and how he came on to her and she had to get away and then the jealousy and unfair accusations and how her cousin still owed her two hundred dollars and FEMA was run by a bunch of morons and the complications her pregnancy had set up with her thyroid problems. Lots of medical bills.

There was an explanation for the missing driver's license too. It seems the policeman who stopped him didn't have probable cause to search his car and the judge threw out the case, but they had already confiscated his license and then they lost it in the storm and "try getting anything at the DMV now. Just try it. They're worse than FEMA and Mayor Nagin combined."

The car was in the shop. The car was being fixed. The guy fixing it was an old buddy—well, the cousin of a buddy—and he agreed to keep the maxed out credit card and only file the claim when given the word that they were back on track. "Hell of a guy. Gave him an old gold chain for collateral. Isn't worth much, but it was something."

Elise just wanted to get out of there. The smell of old fast food garbage, patchouli and what she suspected was marijuana was making her ill. The NASCAR announcer droned on in the background. The air conditioner rattled and groaned and dripped water on the rug. The bed clothes were rumpled and there were clothes and shoes and magazines and overflowing ashtrays and the general atmosphere of chaos and confusion everywhere. What was even more depressing was the fact that these two losers were not hopeless. They exuded a fine mist of optimism. They had plans. They were going to go to Mississippi, get jobs, a house, have that baby, lead a life. The chance of any of those things happening without dozens of more complications and catastrophes was, in Elise's experience, just about zero.

She could see beyond today, something these two young people apparently couldn't. The car would break down again. They would fight. They would get more temporary help. She'd end up in the emergency room again with her thyroid and pregnancy. They'd be in a shelter. He'd find some kind of work. She'd get herself involved with some other man. They'd maybe get a trailer. There would be a fire or a tornado or he'd lose his job. He'd get arrested for driving without a license. They'd find the pot in his car. He'd do some jail time. She'd go off with someone else. Here they were in this motel room in Louisiana smiling at her, hoping for some cash, something tangible they could use right now, ready to feel happy for a moment. He was standing. She was sitting. Elise leaned against the dresser, weighing her options. How much of what they had said was true? She didn't care. If it weren't true, then something else equally bad most certainly was. Right now she could give them a voucher for motel time. She could go pick up some food. She could send them on their way and out of her life and into the kind of mindless cheerful misery that bad decisions, bad taste and bad luck had made for them and probably would always make for them. Elise just wanted to go home, make some tea, look at something that wasn't cheap and ugly and stupid, hear something that wasn't an implausible story or a whine or a complaint, smell something that might possibly be fresh and new.

Elise drove home with the air conditioning going full blast and NPR playing Mozart on the radio. She broke the local law by using her cell phone to call Anthony and begging him to take over for her here and deliver some food to the people at Willow Courts and told him again that she was not the person for this kind of job and he soothed her and got her to agree to think it over and told her he'd take over the rest of the day and to go home and relax.

When she entered her house, she was grateful for the smell of cantaloupe and mango ripening on the counter, grateful for the tasteful artwork, the efficient air conditioning, the modest but stylish furniture, the ceiling fan, the twelve foot ceiling, the excellent stereo system, the comfortable chair and the green tea and the tinkle of wind chimes from her porch.

Even as she told herself that she should make allowances for Katrina, she knew that Katrina was not the biggest problem in those young people's lives. She knew hundreds of Katrina victims. Some were friends. Some had come to St. Vincent for help. Their stories were heartbreaking, but now six months later they had all done something. Their decisions were all over the map. Some had moved away. Some were already rebuilding. Some were still in an emotional limbo. But every one of them was somewhere and this young couple seemed to be nowhere at all, floating, flying, being swept along by forces completely unaware that their own decisions—almost all not so much bad as completely irrelevant—had no effect whatever on the trajectory of their lives, which it seemed to Elise, was nothing more than meaningless, skittish activity.

Elise felt guilty for being so judgmental. She also knew that she had not been so hard on Delinea simply because she was black. Was this a weird kind of racism? She wanted to grab those young people and shake them, something she most definitely did not want to do with Delinea. And what would they think if she spoke her mind? What would they make of this old lady with the long gray braid telling them off? Oh, how she longed to light into them and tell them: "What are you thinking? Are you out of your mind? Can't you see that those tattoos are ugly as sin and make you look cheap and stupid? Lose some weight, girl! And for God's sake, stop eating all that crap from fast food joints! Have you ever heard of a checking account? A dental appointment? A savings plan? Birth control? Making a decision based on something other than what might feel good in the next ten minutes! Do you have even a single friend who isn't a loser? Wake up and smell the coffee!"

They'd think she was crazy. And rude. Too true.

Delinea. Delinea. How much of that story was a big old crock? I forgive you. Good luck.

Well, there was one thing she could do and she did it. She walked to her desk, pulled up her grandson's email and fired off a reply.

"Dear Eric, Sorry about your troubles, but I've decided to give you a great big gift, the biggest thing I own, a piece of advice: Grow up. Take care of yourself. You're twenty-eight years old and should by now be taking care of yourself without grandma having to bail you out. I love you. Keep me posted on how you're doing."

Elise closed down her computer, put her empty teacup in the sink, stood staring out the window at the backyard garden, thought maybe it was time to pick some tomatoes, some cucumbers, some beans. The air conditioning was so cool. The heat shimmered outside, the air dusty with summer, her garden full of vegetables she had providently planted in the spring. She began to cry, not knowing if her tears were for Delinia or the tattooed young couple or her husband who had died in the tomatoes or for her grandson or for herself because she felt for certain that she was nothing but a fool.

CLAIMS AND ADJUSTMENTS

"I have lost my heart." Those were his first words, his first formed words after the screaming and the sobs, when exhaustion had finally, mercifully come, and he could, he found, after all, think. When the emotions had finally drained his mind and body of everything else and he was left only with the empty finality of what he had done. "Nothing in my life will ever be this bad," he thought. He was fourteen years old and he had just killed his twin brother.

It was a story designed to break your heart and the newspapers for once seemed embarrassed at the excess of reality and had no need to sensationalize what was already even in its simple facts an excess of its own.

The twins were not identical, but still were inseparable, each with friends and interests of their own, but ultimately always returning to the other's orbit. It had been that way since they were infants. Barry, the oldest by eight minutes, had been the athletic one, Blue the scholar; but both had shared a love of hunting. At eight years old their father had taken them off to hunt ducks, geese, doves, and deer, and each owned a shotgun, a deer rifle, and a .22 which hung along with their father's guns in a locked oak cabinet in the downstairs hall. Ammunition was in a shoebox in their parents' closet. They had been taught every rule of safety. More important, they loved each other and were, without reservation, good boys. But Barry was a teaser and Blue was in the early adolescent ways of boys too sensitive and not yet able to control the hurt and rage that his brother was able to elicit in the casual, unthinking cruelty of fourteen year olds.

Still, the D.A. was disturbed. If only the gun had been lying out, loaded, ready at hand, an easy appendage to a childish impulse. But no. It was locked away and Blue had to take his Swiss army knife, given to him for Christmas by his grandmother, and pry the door open, splintering the old oak slat. Then he had to walk upstairs, climb onto a chair and pull the shells from the top shelf of his parents' closet, load the gun, and return to the family room and confront his brother.

What was he thinking when he slipped the blade into the door? When he heard the wood splinter softly and the door pop open didn't he know his parents would be appalled at this vandalism? The gun cabinet was, after all, a valuable antique. And then to walk upstairs carefully cradling the shotgun in the crook of his arm, barrel pointing downwards as his father had carefully taught him. What was he thinking? Didn't he know now to stop? Why climb on that chair? (His dusty sneakers had left a careful print on the slip cover.) What was he thinking? Couldn't he stop then, rooting around in the shoeboxes: shoes, shoes, old papers, shoes, finally ammunition including the two boxes of shotgun shells, one new, one already opened, and then taking two shells out of the closely packed box. Why did he need this ammunition? He didn't want to shoot Barry, did he? He had seen things die: ducks, geese, doves, deer. He could fieldstrip, he could butcher, he could cook. Barry? What was he thinking?

"I told him to stop teasing me. Barry and Louis from down the street they just kept on. They were very mean. But I didn't want...(so why did you pry open the cabinet. Why make the long walk upstairs for the shells?)...I didn't want....Barry is my brother. I have lost my heart. I waved the gun at him. I knew it was wrong, but I never really pointed it at him. I pointed it off to the side. But he grabbed the gun. Barry grabbed the gun and it went off. I didn't want...I have lost my heart."

It was a shotgun after all and there was a good deal of blood. Barry was killed instantly, his chest ripped open and his heart and lungs lacerated with the shot.

911. EMT's. Sheriff's deputies. Even a hastily called social worker and the counselor from Blue's school. But through it all from the phone call, "Please hurry. I shot my brother," to the neighbors and the casseroles, his mother held him in a fierce lock and his father between hugs stood in the background and wept. "Hold him, hold him. That's all I thought of," his mother said. "Holding him I was holding them both. Holding them both for the last time."

"I wanted to hate my son's killer," his father said, "but I didn't. I couldn't. I love my son. Nothing is worse than this. For me there is nothing worse and for Blue it is ten times worse. I love my son. I love them both. This is as terrible as it gets. Nothing. Nothing. I love my son."

Finally a pause and Blue has formed the words, lying on the couch, his head on his mother's lap, her fierce grip finally softened. "I have lost my heart." As horrible as her loss, there was another horror. "I have lost my heart." No, no, she thought, you're going to live. I am going to prop you, hold you, protect you. You will not break my heart twice. You are going to live.

Everyone was agonized. At first the D.A. charged Blue with second degree murder. "If only the gun were loaded, easy at hand." At the arraignment the judge released Blue to the custody of his parents, ordered a psychiatric evaluation, continued counseling, and made a prerequisite for his release an assurance that he would never be left alone, never be without an adult present. "I have lost my heart." And then later, "I want to be with my brother." So he was watched. Lawyers huddled with the D.A. The charges were reduced to manslaughter, then to negligent homicide. Everyone wondered, "How do we save this boy?"

Barry and Blue's mother cooks supper. There is venison in the freezer but she has selected pork chops wrapped in cellophane from the A&P. Mashed potatoes, corn on the cob, an onion gravy, a nice green salad with shallots and radishes and snow peas. There's half a left over cake from the neighbors' visitations, the gesture of food for the house in mourning. They sit in silence, a few scattered words, the click of forks on plates.

Blue has gone back to school where the students have been counseled and warned, but where he sits alone and does not ponder the day's lessons but the nail of his thumb, bleeding at the quick, bitten down, skin peeled; he forces a drop of blood onto the neat picture of Chief Tecumseh in his history book and smears the face red. He knows there are living cells in the blood. He has seen them under a microscope in his science class. He wonders how long it will take them to die.

His father has gone to work where his secretary cries and hugs him; his supervisor calls him into his office and shyly suggests if he wants time off....The customers do not know. They come in with their cars damaged and he looks them over and punches buttons and writes checks, assessing damage, adjusting claims, quietly angry at the grief and distress shown by the car owners over the damage to their cars. He doesn't go out to lunch, but sits at his desk and for one hour stares at the swimming fish in the screen saver of his computer: angel fish, angel fish, angel fish, a blue neon thing, angel fish, an orange neon thing, a transparent bony thing, angel fish.

His secretary, Charlotte, has brought him a salad. "You have to eat," she fusses. She is young and pretty, an only child, but knows as if by instinct how to mother, nurse, scold, cajole, and he obediently eats, grazes on the iceberg lettuce, the peppers and carrots. Afterward he does feel better and he attacks the paperwork piled on his desk.

At two o'clock a lady drives in with a Porsche convertible, its top slashed in three places. The estimate says $3000 for a new leather top. She is quiet and careful in her account. Someone has invaded her carport, slashed the top of her husband's new car, only two months old, stolen a camera. She does not seem angry. She is not grieving the desecration of the new car. A small, familiar twinge of suspicion tickles his brain as he slowly circles the car, fingering the neatly sliced leather. He looks at the woman: casual but expensive clothes, hair that is professionally dyed and styled, shoes with matching purse she bought in New York or Dallas, a melancholy smile that is also hiding something. What?

"This is your husband's car?"

"Yes. He has to work. So I brought it in."

"Uh-huh."

"I don't work." She paused and he knew he was going to hear all about it. She smiled and cleared her throat. "I have a master's degree in social work. I used to work at the hospital. That's where I met my husband. He's a doctor, you know?"

"Oh?"

"Yes. Everyone loves him." She suddenly laughed at the absurdity of people. "Do you see this?" She pulled up the silk sleeve of her blouse. He thought he was going to see bruises, but instead she fingered a delicate diamond tennis bracelet that circled her thin wrist. "He bought me this. It's my consolation prize."

"For not getting a new car?"

She laughed. "No, no. I don't care about cars. It's my husband who cares about cars." Suddenly she began to cry. He stood quietly, embarrassed at her public display. "I am sorry," she said. "I shouldn't have come."

"I haven't filled out a claim. You haven't yet done anything wrong."

Her sobs continued and she began to beat on the car with her fists. She kicked at the driver's door and managed to put in two ugly dents before he grabbed her. She stopped struggling and looked at him. "You want to help me, don't you? I know who you are. It is not fair what happened to your son. Help me finish off this car." She managed one more kick at the fender.

All he could say was, "Shhh. Shhh. Calm down. How about if we go in and sit down?" Finally she allowed him to lead her inside. "Don't call anyone," she said. "I will be fine." Charlotte brought them coffee and they sat quietly sipping in his office. He was incredibly calm, even happy. The clock ticked. Outside the phone rang and he could hear Charlotte's muffled voice answering it.

He looked at the woman as she delicately sipped her coffee from the insurance company mug. She was younger than he had at first thought. No more than forty, perhaps even thirty-five. It was the clothes that had fooled him. The silk blouse, the flowing pants, the look of casual elegance and money. She would look better in jeans and a t-shirt, he thought. She would be more comfortable.

"Have you ever felt as if your life was over?" she asked.

He flashed out of the corner of his mind's eye his twin sons playing ball in the backyard and then his wife holding Blue. "I have lost my heart." Heat flowed up behind his breastbone and he suddenly hated this woman and her stupid marriage problems. She went on. "My troubles are nothing like yours. I apologize. It's just that they're mine and I must tend to them." He suddenly remembered reading a newspaper story about a fire in Illinois where a man came home to find three of his children dead. He had read the story sitting at the kitchen table and he felt guilty for being sad about something—what was it?—an argument with his wife. Something stupid. Who knows? But then the story faded and he was in his own life again, looking up at his wife's long legs and the curve of her hip and feeling desire rise in him like mercury. He suddenly thought. We haven't made love since Barry died. He wanted this woman to go away. He wanted Charlotte to bring him a cup of tea, some cinnamon toast and comfort. He wanted to lie on his queen sized bed at home under the ceiling fan and feel his wife's lips over his body and to think of nothing. But he could hear the woman talking.

"My mother told me that God does not send troubles too big for you to handle. The bigger the troubles, the stronger you must be in God's eyes. I guess that makes you a Superman and me a weakling. I'm unhappy and I have no reason. I've become one of those rich bitches I always hated when I was in school and when I worked at the hospital. The doctors' wives who dressed so fine and spent all their money on personal trainers and color consultants and furniture. Who drove around all day in a Mercedes delivering children to piano lessons and soccer games. But Doug seemed so different. He really is a dedicated doctor. Then after I got married I found out. All those women became my friends. All their husbands—well, most of them, anyway—are dedicated doctors. That's the problem really. They're doctors before they're anything else. I am sorry. I shouldn't have come."

"What will you tell your husband?"

"I don't know."

"Will he be angry?"

"He is not abusive if that's what you mean."

"No. I just wondered...."

"I will be all right. I am terribly sorry about your son."

She stood and offered him her hand. She held his hand for a moment and as if deciding something very important put her other hand up in the air in a gesture that was unsure of what it wanted to do. Her hand paused in midair, palm out toward him, hesitated between options, so many possibilities—a caress, a policeman's emphatic stop, a public speaker's call for emphasis—and in its awkward eloquence she looked at him intently. "It is very important for you to believe that my mother was right. God does not send troubles too big for us to handle. She was right. You are blessed." She paused and her strength wavered, her eyes became shy and fell to the ground; her hand now seemed an awkward non-gesture. She let go of his hand, turned. "Thank you," she said and had opened the door and was walking away before he could respond.

Charlotte came into the room. "You had two calls," she said, handing him a slip of paper. "The other caller was your wife. There was no message. Nothing important. She said to tell you she loves you."

"Thank you."

"I've made you some tea."

"Thank you."

"I can take care of this. I know what to do," she said, reaching for the telephone memo paper.

"No, no, I'm all right. I can do it. Thank you for the tea."

"That woman. She did it herself, didn't she?"

"Yes."

"I knew she did. I could tell when she first got out of the car."

He worked all afternoon, concentrating on the paper, carefully and gratefully emptying his In Box and filling his Out Box. He couldn't remember being so organized, so efficient, so careful and quick in his assessments. At five o'clock he felt a tiny rush of happy satisfaction. He had even cleaned the top of his desk. He stood to go. As he slipped on his jacket Charlotte handed him a Tupperware container shyly. "It's a cake. I baked it myself. It's Italian cream. Everybody loves it. I put the recipe inside in case your wife wants to try it sometime. I hope you like it."

"Thank you, Charlotte. That is so sweet."

"I know that cooking…well, sometimes it's difficult."

"Yes. Thank you."

He drove slowly. It seemed as if every leaf and twig was outlined in light. Could he be feeling happiness? His stomach grumbled and he realized that he was hungry. No breakfast, only the salad for lunch. Suddenly the thought of the rich cake beside him made him long for a really big supper. He was driving down a one way street, tree lined with overarching oaks and large homes and small businesses. Just as he passed the back parking lot of the Jacmel Inn he saw a large turtle in the other lane making his slow deliberate way across the street.

He thought: I should go help him. He could be hit by a car. The thought of death stabbed him again behind the sternum and he drove on thinking he had enough troubles of his own without quixotic attempts to save a stupid turtle's life. But two blocks later he turned left, then turned left again and made his way to the main entrance of Jacmel. He pulled into the parking lot and drove into the other side, parked and got out. He walked to the street and saw that the turtle had made his way to the center line where he was paused as if wondering what to do next. He must have been terrified by the inexplicable rush of cars. It was a miracle he was alive. But perhaps people avoided him. Several cars rushed by and the man paused, waiting for a break in the traffic before he could walk into the street, scoop up the turtle and take him to the other side. What was so important on the other side that the turtle was so determined to go there? A ditch, a large lawn, some trees. No better than this side. He could see a break in the traffic up ahead. Two cars, a third, a rusty red pickup, and then he could go. The three cars drove by. As the pickup approached he heard its driver let out a yell. The pickup swerved toward the center line and with a sickening metallic clink and crunch he hit the turtle crushing its shell. The driver and his passenger laughed and sped up.

The man could see the dead turtle upside down twenty feet away and several large chunks of shell scattered about. How did this happen? He thought. He didn't remember kneeling down, but here he was kneeling in the sharp shells of the restaurant driveway. His pants were ripped and he felt blood trickling down his shin.

He felt rage, a hot flush of consuming rage, and then a calm, cold, certain determination that seemed to be desperation. He rose, walked to his car, sped out of the parking lot with a crunching squeal of tires and set off in pursuit of the assholes that he felt completely justified in exterminating from a world they did not deserve. It took two miles and some speeding, but there they were up ahead of him. Now that he saw the pickup he wondered: What am I going to do? What if they keep on driving? What if they stop? And then they did. They pulled into a convenience store and parked. There were three of them packed into the cab.

He parked on the other side and walked toward them. They were still laughing. Drunk? The driver was a big man in a brown t-shirt and had more tattoos than teeth. The middle passenger was a woman with doughy white complexion, sharp features, and acne scarred skin. She was smoking a cigarette and running her fingers through her thin, greasy brown hair. The other man was also thin and very short, almost a dwarf, and walked with a limp. All three were wearing dirty blue jeans and tennis shoes caked with gray, powdery clay.

"Excuse me. Wait a minute. Excuse me." What am I doing? he thought. These people could be crazy. Certainly they were violent. But he had to know. He had to understand. How could a person deliberately kill a living thing like that? Do they actually get pleasure from it? How could they do it?

"I have to know," he said. "I have to know."

They stood staring at him—open faced, smiling, expecting, no doubt, to be asked directions to the interstate or something. Friendly. Open. Helpful. Dumb as dirt. Even innocent. Asking them why would be like asking a plant to explain photosynthesis. He felt tears on his cheeks.

"Are you OK, mister?" the little guy asked.

"Do you know that your knee is bleeding?" the woman asked.

"I have to know. Why did you deliberately kill that turtle?"

"You're crying over a turtle?" the big guy asked.

"Shit. He's crazy," the little guy said, and he shifted his weight, anticipating what might happen next.

"Does it give you pleasure to kill like that?"

The woman stuck her little finger in her ear and vibrated it back and forth. "Come on. Leave him alone, fellows."

The big guy took a step forward. "No. I want to know where he gets off worrying about a damn turtle. What's it to you, asshole? Was it your turtle or something?"

"You do not deserve to live." He said it with conviction. He knew it wasn't true, but he wanted it to be true. He wanted to have a weapon. The big guy pushed him in the chest with his finger.

"What did you say?"

The woman grabbed the big guy's arm. The little guy moved off to the side and an object appeared in his hand. A box cutter. The big guy pushed.

"Put that thing away, Floyd. Don't be stupid," the woman said to the little guy. And then there were four things that happened very fast. The big guy pushed hard. The father threw a punch that landed on the big guy's ear. The big guy hit him twice—once full in the face and once as he was going down, glancing off his shoulder. The woman pulled the big guy away. He shook her off but that was only for show. He was finished.

"Leave him alone. He's crazy," she said.

The father knelt in the parking lot. His knee hurt. His nose hurt. He felt blood on his face. He was flush with adrenaline and then he was empty. Two teenage boys stopped and looked down at him.

"You OK?"

"Yes." And he realized that the big guy, the little guy, and the woman were gone. The red pickup was no longer in the parking lot.

"You better see to that nose. It looks broken."

"Yes. I'll do that."

"What happened?"

"I don't know."

The teenagers walked into the store. He saw them talking to the Vietnamese man behind the counter. They were looking out at him. He got up and walked to his car, dabbing at his nose with his handkerchief. On the driver's side door he saw that someone had run a sharp object (a box cutter?) back and forth in what looked like a child's scribble.

In the emergency room parking lot he called his wife on his cell phone and told her he would be late. Then he lifted the Tupperware top off the cake and delicately ran his finger along the bottom edge and licked the sweet, comforting icing off his finger. He noticed his knuckles were bleeding and his ring finger was bent and swollen. There were damages. Physical damages. And pain and suffering. He would have to make a claim. He would have to make an adjustment.

ACCELERANT

Bernie wasn't expecting the question. He imagined the police officer might ask all kinds of questions and he was prepared. Tell the truth. Tell the absolute truth about everything except, of course, for the one little detail that he had to lie about, the one little detail that yes, he had in fact started the fire. Otherwise, tell the truth. About everything. Where he was. At the casino. How he felt about it? Good. Insurance? Of course. He never expected the question the police officer asked.

"Bernie," the cop asked, "do you have any cats?"

"Cats?"

"Yeah. Cats. You got any cats?"

Bernie knew his goose was cooked. What could he say? He told them the truth, the damning truth. "No. No cats."

As it turned out there were other things. Little details. Forensics. There's always something. But when the fire investigator told the jury about the gasoline soaked kitty litter that had been the accelerant, that about did it. Bernie was convicted of arson and was sent up for a five year sentence. That changed everything. Arson meant no insurance. No insurance meant he lost his business. And his girlfriend. And his freedom.

In Louisiana only the worst criminals get sent to Angola and he hardly qualified for that. What he did was what lots of folks did—"creative refinancing" is what they called it, but the law called it arson and he got five years in the B.B. "Sixty" Rayburn Correctional Facility, the medium security prison outside Bogalusa, where if the wind was right you could smell the paper mill. "How do they stand it in town?" Bernie wondered. The smell was worse than a sewer.

Then he was out after three and a half years what with good behavior and the need for more room for new guys coming in. He left the prison with no idea in his head what in the world he was going to do. He was thirty-eight years old. No job. No family. No prospects. No ideas. He bought himself a beer and some barbeque potato chips and caught a bus to New Orleans.

Sometimes things just happen. That's the truth. So Bernie was pleased in a way, but not really surprised when the very first night of his freedom he got lucky. That's what he and his friends, his ex-friends now, used to say, "Got lucky," as in "Did you get lucky this weekend?" "So how'd the date go? You get lucky?" "Was it a good party? Did you get lucky?"

The girl was a waitress. No, not a waitress, although she did bus the few tables in the place and she did take orders under the sign "Place Orders Here" and deliver the orders under the sign that said "Pickup Orders Here." She worked in a donut shop and Bernie was drinking hot chocolate and eating three donuts, one glazed, one chocolate, one Bavarian cream. He had come in for a coffee, but then decided on hot chocolate instead. He had drunk coffee every day in prison, but it had been three and a half years since he had had hot chocolate. It sounded good. He couldn't remember if the prison had ever served any donuts, but he was pretty sure it hadn't.

He was sitting in a booth drinking his hot chocolate and eating his donuts when he heard the girl arguing with the guy in the back who was making the donuts. It wasn't hard to hear them because they were both yelling pretty loud. Their voices got angrier and then the cursing started and there was the sound of metal hitting something else metal and then the girl said "Fuck you, A.J. I quit!"

Next thing you know the girl was in the front throwing off her paper hat, then she pulled off her donut shop uniform top and was standing there in her bra and she pulled off her pants and threw them down too and then she grabbed a coat off the rack, one of those heavy, puffy coats with a fake fur collar and she put it on and she headed for the door. The coat only came to the top of her thighs and Bernie could see she had terrific legs.

Bernie got up and carried his hot chocolate outside. He almost ran into the guy from the back who was opening the door as Bernie got to it. The guy was middle aged, had a little mustache and needed a shave. He had a pot belly and round cheeks like he must eat donuts all the time.

He yelled a few choice curses at the girl who was about to get into her car and the girl gave him the finger without looking back. Bernie stood there drinking his hot chocolate and the guy went back into the shop without saying anything to Bernie. Bernie watched the girl back up her car out of the parking spot and turn toward him. She saw him standing there. He grinned at her.

"You got quite a mouth," Bernie says. The girl looked at him, sizing him up, wondering what to do with him. Bernie thought she was going to say "fuck you" or "thanks." He was not sure which, but what she did say was, "You want to get in?"

Bernie grinned some more. "Yes," he said, "yes, I want to get in."

Two weeks later Bernie was still in the girl's apartment, sitting on her broken down, stained couch patched with duct tape and drinking his third beer of the night. "Packaging," Bernie thought to himself. He almost said it out loud. Then he did say it out loud. "Packaging. It's all about packaging." He was beginning to get what he thought might be an idea. The girl, a girl Bernie now reluctantly thought of as "my girlfriend," was at work. She had the late shift at the airport shining shoes. She wouldn't be off until ten o'clock, another three hours, and then she'd probably stop off somewhere for a couple of beers or a daiquiri. She wouldn't be home until midnight at the earliest, not that Bernie cared. If anything, he preferred being alone. In prison he was never alone and he didn't realize how much he missed it until he had a chance to have a few hours to himself. It felt great. He wanted more of it. He wanted to get rid of the girlfriend. He wanted to move out. He wanted to be alone for awhile. Trouble was he had nowhere else to go. She was paying for everything including his cigarettes and beer. Where would he go? What would he do?

"Packaging," he said again, louder this time. He shook his head. "It sure as hell sold me." He was thinking back to the night he met Angel (that was the girl's name.) When she stripped off her donut shop shirt and stood there in her bra his heart flopped. When she dropped her pants he forgot to chew the donut that was congealing in his mouth. But when she put on that coat, the coat that just barely reached beyond her crotch and she walked out the door he stopped breathing. It was just so sexy. It was so…perfect.

Even when he stared at her face in the car he didn't really see her. He was still seeing those legs reaching up, up, up to the edge of that coat. Later that night he saw all of her, her whole body up above him bouncing up and down on top of him and he had to admit her body was pretty damned good. He hadn't had a woman in almost four years, but it wasn't just that. She really had a nice body. Maybe not perfect. Maybe there was a little too much thickness around the waist. Maybe there was a little to be desired in the bosom department. But nice. Still nice.

It was her face that was the problem. There was nothing wrong with any one feature. Eyes OK. Nose OK. Mouth OK. Maybe a bit lacking in the chin department, but only a little. Everything was OK. It's just that put all together they didn't add up to anything. Plain. That's what she was. And her complexion wasn't so great either.

She must have known she needed a little enhancement because she had dyed her hair blonde some time ago, but the dark roots were clearly visible. She also piled on the makeup which probably explained the breakouts here and there. Her lips were sexy, bright, bright red, but they didn't make her look good, only available, showing off, you know how that works.

He had tried to work up the courage to ask her to get naked and then put on that coat. "Packaging," he thought, "God bless packaging."

Here was his idea. Angel had told him that there were guys in the airport who would choose her over old Timothy or even Gwen because she was "cute." That's what she said, "cute," but Bernie didn't correct her. Anyway, he knew what she meant. The guys getting their shoes shined would sit on these chairs a couple steps up and Angel would be leaning over down below by their feet and Angel always wore those low cut t-shirts and push-up bras turning what little breasts she had into nice little mounds. The guys liked that.

So Bernie figured why not franchise? Why not get a bunch of girls, girls prettier and more endowed than Angel. Give them a snazzy, sexy uniform and set them up with shoe shine stands? It could be a gold mine. He hadn't mentioned his idea to Angel yet and he wasn't sure how she'd like it, but he was pretty sure she'd go for it. How could it lose?

Of course he'd need some startup money. And maybe he'd start small. One or two stands in the obvious places. Maybe set up in hotel lobbies. He wasn't sure how to go about this. He also wasn't sure if he'd need licenses or permits or anything if he set up on public properties like sidewalks or outside restaurants or clubs. "Packaging," he said out loud again. "It's all about packaging."

He was on his fifth beer and watching the rerun of a basketball game he didn't care about when Angel got home. It was almost one o'clock.

"Hey," she said.

"Hey." He could tell she was drunk. He could also tell she was in the mood for a fight. No use bringing up his idea now. Whatever he said she would laugh at it, say it was stupid.

"Still drinking my beer, I see," she said.

"Yeah," he said, ignoring that crack about "my" beer.

"I saw somebody tonight," she said.

"Yeah? Who?"

"A guy."

"What guy?"

"Just a guy. He was a guy who had a job. We talked, laughed, had a few beers. Good looking guy too."

"Yeah?"

"If you hadn't been here, I would've brought him home."

"Oh yeah?"

"Yeah, I would have."

"Why didn't you go to his place?"

"Maybe I did," she said in a way that he knew meant she hadn't. She was just trying to get a rise out of him. She wanted a fight. She wanted to yell and be mad. She liked that.

It gave her pleasure. They had already gone through that scenario several times before he caught on. She'd pick a fight, there would be a screaming match and next thing you knew they'd be rolling around in the bed and she'd pull his clothes off, cursing him the whole time and then melt into a needy little girl begging him to give her pleasure.

The first time it happened Bernie was excited. The next time scared him. Was this chick crazy? Then it became a drag. He didn't want it anymore. He wanted out. So he wouldn't give her the satisfaction of getting mad.

She looked at him with contempt. "You don't even care, do you?" she said.

He shrugged, not trusting his voice because he really was angry now.

"You are a poor excuse for a man, you know that?" she said.

He didn't say anything out loud, but inside he was saying plenty.

Packaging is a funny thing. When she was half naked under that puffy coat in the donut shop she was desirable, stunning even. Now, standing there in the living room in the same puffy coat but with baggy workpants and men's shoes, her head covered in that stupid stocking cap she was ugly. She was mean and she was ugly and she stood there trying to hurt him, trying to make him mad.

She looked even uglier when she followed him into the kitchen where he went to get his sixth beer. Even uglier when she pulled off that stupid hat and her dried up half blonde hair stuck out at all angles from the static electricity. She had a big zit on her chin. Her lipstick was gone. When she opened her mouth to insult him he could see her bad teeth, see the one missing on the lower left.

"In case you haven't noticed," she said, "*I* have a *job*. Have you ever looked for a job? Have you even lifted a finger around here? One little finger? Hell, all you do is sit around all day watching the damned TV and drinking *my* beer. You are one sorry old loser, that's for sure. I don't know why I let you into my car. What was I thinking? Story of my life. One damned loser after another. I deserve better than this."

She went on. The usual. He got his beer, ignored her, walked back into the living room. She followed him. He turned around and walked back into the kitchen, grabbed an open bag of Cheetos off the counter, returned to the living room. She followed him, still talking. He was trying to remain calm. He walked back into the kitchen. She followed, continuing to talk. "I get home, I'm *exhausted*. And there you are sitting on your ass. I know you. You're thinking I'll be glad to see you. Give you a big kiss. Sit on your lap all lovey-dovey...."

When he hit her she went down and she scooted across the floor, her back against the counter. He stood over her with his hands in fists and his teeth clenched. She looked up at him, surprised, even a little bit frightened. She said, "Baby," and now he was frightened. He had never in his life hit a woman. In fact, except for that fight with Jason Doherty in middle school, he had never hit anyone. She crawled over to him and stayed kneeling in front of him, looking up. He could see a red splotch on her chin and a trickle of blood from the corner of her mouth.

Sometimes you just have to decide. You just have to. But he couldn't. He couldn't decide. And so when she pulled herself up, when she cradled his head, when she said, "Baby, baby" and "it's OK, it's OK," he let her. He let her do it. There were other things he could have done. He knew that. He wasn't stupid. But he knew he wouldn't do them. He knew that all right. So he let her. It's OK, he thought. It's only for now. It's OK.

LISTENING TO MUSIC

Downstairs in the living room my friend Louis was pouring himself yet another scotch. From the bed in Louis's guest bedroom I could hear the clink of ice cubes, the pause as he poured and sipped and the longer pause as he went to his stereo, pushed the buttons, adjusted the volume, and then the first strains of Dvorak's New World Symphony. I dreaded what I knew would happen next. It was always the same. The ice. The scotch. The music. And then Louis would begin to weep.

The recording had been made earlier in the evening. Louis had conducted the university's symphony orchestra and he had been sure, absolutely sure that this time the performance was brilliant. When it was over he was all smiles as he asked the orchestra to rise, shook hands with the concertmaster, bowed to the audience's standing ovation. He was completely happy. Now he was listening to what the audience heard and as he realized once again (he never learned) the horrible truth of his orchestra's shortcomings, he once again began to cry.

Across the hall in the bathroom there was the sound of the faucet being turned on and then off. Louis's wife, Marjorie, was getting ready for bed. She too had come upstairs early to escape. It was what Louis wanted anyway. No matter how late we stayed up, he would wait for us to leave before reliving his triumph by playing the recording. Only it was never what he expected. It was always the same. The ice. The scotch. The stereo. The weeping as the truth became clear. I wondered how Marjorie could stand it.

My ex-wife never liked Louis. It wasn't why we got divorced, but it didn't help. Louis was a constant in my life, my oldest and best friend, even though he didn't make it easy to be friends with him. "He's going to drive you crazy," she said, "He's going to hurt you. Can't you see that?"

I did see that. But I couldn't help it. I didn't think I had a choice. We had known each other since high school in New Orleans when we played in the marching band, Louis the trumpet and me the far less glamorous trombone. He was always pointing that out to me. "The trombone?" he said. "Don't you know the chicks go for trumpet players? Trombones are for geeks."

It was the same in the local college where we both majored in music. He, of course, was a trumpet performance major and I went into the once again far less glamorous field of music education. The thing is Louis was really good. I mean really good. I was good, but I feared, rightfully so as it turned out, that I would never be able to make a living as a trombone player. Far more practical, if also less glamorous, to aim for teaching high school kids how to march on a football field.

After college we kept in touch, a lot more than I had anticipated, if truth be told. I got on at a high school on the north shore and rose in less than five years to band director, got married, settled down for what looked like the duration and he did the far more glamorous thing, hitchhiking across Europe and India and then getting gigs in increasingly more prestigious orchestras, finally ending up in St. Louis, and, in a short time, he was principal trumpet.

We'd talk on the phone, send letters. Every now and then we'd get together, sometimes here at home in Louisiana when he visited his father (his mother was dead), a couple times in St. Louis timed to catch a concert and a ball game. Every time he had a different girl and as he grew older, the girls stayed the same, twenty-year-old music students full of admiration and hormones.

That changed one summer when his father died. During the visit home for the funeral he met Marjorie, a home town girl older than his usual conquests, but still bright and sexy at thirty-five. She wasn't just older. She was absolutely nothing like Louis. For one thing she had no interest whatever in classical music or any music at all really. And even though she was undoubtedly attractive ("a pretty girl," my wife said, "he really doesn't deserve her,") she was also down to earth and practical and completely devoid of drama and glamour. She was a nurse who worked for a pediatric oncologist and she never ever talked about her work.

"I think Louis is smitten," I told my wife.

"Poor girl," she said.

Over the next six months Louis collected a lot of frequent flyer miles flying in to New Orleans to see Marjorie. It must have worked because eight months after they met they were married and Marjorie moved to St. Louis. Within a year Marjorie's father was diagnosed with pancreatic cancer and a month later her mother was diagnosed with the early stages of Alzheimer's. Marjorie was pregnant with their first child.

For Marjorie it was non-negotiable. She insisted they move back to be near her parents and Louis finally agreed. I don't know if it was love or just her implacable will that did it, but Louis was no match for her even though he must have hated moving away from his home and the job he loved. In some ways he was lucky. He got on at the University of New Orleans as an adjunct professor and even though he lacked the proper degree it wasn't long before they gave him a tenured position and a few years and two more children later he was the director and conductor of the university orchestra.

In the final stages of her father's disease and the early stages of her mother's dementia Marjorie virtually lived in their house, cooking all their meals and supervising their care. She kept her job, even visited the gym and tai chi classes during it all. When her father died, it did not register with her mother who was always asking for him. "Where is he?" she would ask. "He was right here a minute ago." Marjorie moved her mother into her house and hired round the clock nurses. That's when the crying started.

Another friend of mine explained it. Bernie was band director at a rival high school. We had the same job but not the same ambitions. I was pretty confident I was where I was supposed to be. I still liked, even if I didn't love, the trombone. I enjoyed teaching. I knew I was doing some good and I was mostly happy. Bernie had been a performance major. Saxophone. He was sure he was every bit as good as Charlie Parker. He was sure he was going to make it and become a jazz icon. He didn't and after four years of infrequent gigs, temp work and ramen noodles, he went back to school, got his education credentials and started teaching band in high school

"Here's what you have to understand about conductors," Bernie said. "There are two kinds. One kind doesn't really hear what's right in front of him. He's conducting away and the kids are playing, but what he hears is the New York Philharmonic. He hears what's supposed to be there. These people are deluded but happy. Then there's the second type. They hear with exaggerated intensity what the kids are actually playing—and of course what they're playing isn't very good. All he can hear are the mistakes, the not very good. These people are miserable."

"I don't know," I said. "I think I hear what they're playing and some of it's good and some of it isn't. And anyway, you have to judge them on their own basis. They're not going to be the New York Philharmonic. That's crazy. But they're not bad either."

"Yes, they are. They're bad. Really bad."

"So you're miserable?" I asked.

"Pretty much," he said.

Louis was cursed because he heard both. While he was conducting the kids he heard the St. Louis Symphony in his head. He was still there, the big fish with the big professional orchestra and as long as he was conducting he was supremely happy. He'd come home full of adrenaline and smiles still hearing the enthusiastic applause, basking in the glory of the inevitable standing ovation. He would hit the scotch bottle (I always thought he had a drinking problem, something he vehemently and predictably denied) and he'd talk nonstop about how glorious the music was, how lucky he was to make a living doing what he loved. And then Marjorie would go to bed. She had to get up early. She had to face a day of dying children. And he would refill his glass and punch the buttons on his stereo and listen to the concert that had made him so happy. And then he would hear what really was there. Not the clear and powerful sounds of the St. Louis Symphony but the struggling work of some undergraduate amateurs. Every wrong note, every slur, every mistake, every time even when they were correct but uninspired would be like a hammer to his temple. "No good. No good. No good. I am so stupid." And he would begin to cry.

Upstairs, Marjorie could hear his sobs, hear the tinkle of ice in the glass even above the strains of Dvorak, and she would weep with him, sure that any comfort she tried to give him would only increase his pain, convince him she felt not respect or understanding or even love, but only pity and perhaps some guilt for dragging him away from the place he loved, where there was real music, music you could believe in, home to this godforsaken town and these no talent students and this agony.

He never learned.

Every concert was the same. He was sure this time he had heard them for real and true. It was good. It really was. Maybe not professional. Maybe not that. But the kids got it. They responded to him. They played their hearts out. This time he was sure. And then the drinking, the click of the stereo and the horrible truth would emerge along with the tears.

As I lay in the bed upstairs hearing the kids play Dvorak about as well as kids could, I tried not to hear the tears, the cursing, the tinkling ice cubes, the cries of "Oh no, come on," and "Can't you count for God's sake?" But I couldn't help it. I heard it all.

The first time I visited Louis to attend his concert I was surprised when Marjorie said she was going to bed. True, Louis was on his way to drunk, red in the face and expansive, but he was so happy and he had just announced he was going to play the concert back. "A little post-mortem," he said and he laughed. Marjorie was picking up the plates of snacks and she gestured for me to help her bring them into the kitchen. Standing over the sink she whispered to me, "Go to bed. He wants to be alone to listen."

"Are you sure?" I asked.

"Trust me. Really."

And so I told Louis I was really tired and I would see him in the morning. "OK, buddy," he said, "I'm just too pumped to sleep."

"It was really good, Louis."

"Oh yeah," he said, "not bad, not bad at all."

The guest bedroom was at the top of the stairs, a wide room across from the bathroom. The bed was covered with an old comforter, a satin pillow embroidered with the words "St. Louis, Gateway to the West." There was an enormous poster advertising the St. Louis Symphony, a concert from twenty years ago. The poster announced my friend Louis as the featured soloist. On the opposite wall were high school graduation pictures of Louis's three children, two girls and a boy, all smiling at the camera. In my ex-house, my ex-wife had pictures just like these of our own kids.

I was ten years divorced and no longer living in my home town. My wife says she couldn't take my unhappiness, my self-pity, my lack of ambition. I don't know. Maybe she was right. Now she is remarried to someone who is very ambitious and by all accounts she's miserable. So maybe she wasn't.

I didn't expect anything that first time I visited for a concert. I was still wondering why Marjorie had been so insistent I go to bed and leave Louis alone downstairs, but then I heard the music start and a moment later I was appalled to hear Louis crying. I didn't know what to do. I finally decided I owed it to my friend to go downstairs and see him… see what I could do.

He was not happy to see me. He was obviously embarrassed, not by his tears, but by the music that was coming out of the stereo. "Why didn't you tell me?" he asked. "Why didn't you tell me how awful it was?"

I tried to convince him it wasn't awful. It was kids, university students, not all of them even music majors. They did a good job. He had to be realistic. None of it worked. He felt betrayed. He cursed me, accused me of pitying him, laughing at him behind his back. Finally he told me to just go away. "I have to," he said, "but there's no reason you have to listen to this shit." I went back upstairs.

The next morning at breakfast he seemed to have forgotten the things he said to me. He was hung over, depressed and very quiet. Marjorie talked about her garden and the hummingbirds that fluttered around the tall bottlebrush plants outside the dining room window. I stayed as long as politeness dictated and then I left.

A year later he invited me again to come hear his concert. He was cheerful, enthusiastic even and he wouldn't take no for an answer. I didn't want to, but I went. That time I didn't need Marjorie to tell me I should go to bed before he played the recording of the concert. I heard the crying, but I didn't go downstairs.

He never learned. It was an annual trial, a trial of our friendship, a trial of my loyalty. And it was always the same. Happy anticipation. Concert. Standing ovation. Scotch. Music. Tears. And the next morning a subdued Louis amidst the perfect scrambled eggs, the green onions, the sausage and the toast and jam, the French drip coffee and the fresh squeezed juice, the cloth napkins and the morning sun. There he would sit, his back to the window, his thinning hair haloed in the dawn and behind him the hummingbirds, oblivious, sucked the sweet nectar from the deep red flowers of the bottlebrush plants and Marjorie, so familiar with suffering, readied herself for work.

On that last day, the last time I accepted his invitation, the last time I slept in that comfortable guest bedroom with the homemade comforter and the "St. Louis Gateway to the West" satin pillow, Louis arose from the breakfast table, his eggs untouched and announced he was going to his office. After he left Marjorie cleaned up and I helped, making small talk until she stood, back to me, leaning over the dishwasher, head down and I was afraid she might be crying.

"How can you stand it?" I asked.

She turned to me and I was surprised to see her eyes were dry and she had on her face, not a look of stricken grief, but one of quiet determination. She even smiled.

"Do you know what I'm thinking of?" she asked.

"No," I said, afraid of what she might tell me.

"Mr. Granderson," she said.

I looked at her blankly.

"He's the grandpa," she said. "His granddaughter is his heart and his granddaughter has no hope, no hope at all. What I'm thinking about is how he does have hope. There isn't a reason in the world why he should and someday very soon he's going to know that. I'm going to see him today and he's going to be nice. He's a very nice man. And when he shows me his goddamned hope I will want to scream. But I won't. I won't scream because that's my job. My job—every day—is to keep from screaming. That's what I do."

There was a silence. Once again I was afraid she was going to cry, but she didn't.

"You want some more coffee?" she asked.

"No. No, thank you. I should be going."

"Yes," she said. "Yes, me too."

THE LAST HAND

Scene One: The Three Piece Suit

Harrison Campbell turned fourteen years old on September 2, 1965. He received several birthday presents, but the main gift, the one he had requested, was a light weight gray three piece suit. Included in the large box that contained the suit were three shirts, two white and one blue, and three brand new ties. Two days later he wore the suit on his first day of high school and sealed forever his image among his classmates as "a queer duck."

Scene Two: The Summer after the Summer of Love

The summer after his high school graduation, Harrison did what he thought of as "a very American thing." He went on a road trip. Since he didn't own a car he was forced to consider how he might recruit a partner in this enterprise, a partner who could drive. There was only one candidate.

All throughout his four years of high school, Harrison had (to put it mildly) "not fit in." Since he wasn't obviously effeminate and since he didn't fit into any established group that elicited the hatred of any other group, he was not bullied or even ostracized. He was simply ignored. The big wheels on campus like the athletes, cheerleaders and student council types ignored him. But so did all the usual outcasts like the hippies, nerds and troublemakers. There was only one boy, Clarence Antin, who was every bit as isolated and *sui generis* as Harrison. And he had a car.

If truth be told they had almost nothing in common. Harrison was an A student in the college prep classes and Clarence scraped by in the vo-tech curriculum. They were aware, of course, that they were both homosexual, but they had never broached the subject and were not in the least attracted to each other. They were both virgins. But Clarence had a car and he also had a great desire to go to San Francisco. He wanted to go to Fillmore West and hear Gracie Slick.

Harrison, while he was very much attracted to bohemia, he was not in the least interested in Haight-Ashbury. He despised the music. He despised the politics. He was a student of the nineteenth century American transcendentalism and while he recognized the radicalism of his hero, Thoreau (he delighted in pronouncing the name correctly— "thorough", not "the row" and loved to correct people), he also realized that Thoreau's politics were really a radical conservativism which became his lifelong creed and while he saw early on that the Vietnam war was a ridiculous and wasteful enterprise, he thought the hippies and peaceniks were equally ridiculous. When he thought of bohemia he thought of the 1920s in Paris and Greenwich Village. Parisian bohemia was no doubt long dead and perhaps the same was true of Greenwich Village, but nostalgia and hope had motivated Harrison to apply to NYU, where he was accepted and he was impatient to get there and see what he could see. In the meantime, however, Clarence had a car and Clarence was going to San Francisco.

They stocked the car with a case of Falstaff beer, an ounce of marijuana and a carton of Chesterfield cigarettes and headed west. For the first time in his life Harrison passed out of Louisiana and crossed Texas, New Mexico and Arizona before entering California and then headed north along Highway 1 toward the city by the bay. In between stops to see the sights (Houston, the Grand Canyon, Carlsbad Caverns, Santa Fe), the two of them confessed their not so secret secret and laughed and enjoyed talking about their various crushes on movie stars and fellow students. They also tentatively discussed their fantasies and made even more tentative hints that perhaps it was time ("fate" is what they called it) to lose their cherries, which they did in a motel in the middle of Texas where they first talked and talked and then asked and answered and finally enthusiastically tried out everything they had been dreaming about since puberty before retreating to their separate beds.

Clarence loved San Francisco, but for Harrison it was pretty much a bust. They repeated their sexual experiments one more time on the way back, their last night in Lafayette, Louisiana and the next day when Clarence dropped Harrison off at his home, Harrison's last words were "see you", which proved to be false because Harrison went off to New York and Clarence, at his father's insistence enrolled in LSU where he flunked out and a year later he was dead, a car accident in the streets of Saigon.

Scene Three: God Laughs

Harrison loved everything about New York and especially Greenwich Village. He majored in English at NYU and soon discovered that his love affair with nineteenth century American transcendentalism was but a naïve youthful mistake. The real heart of his soul lay elsewhere—in the eighteenth century rationalism that was a more serious, mature, and ultimately truthful and consistent basis for a philosophy of life, esthetic, and lifestyle that fit perfectly with the person he had become. He bought a new three piece suit more appropriate for the New York winters. He read Samuel Johnson and Hobbes. He searched for verities and he found them. He also made some friends and discovered that eccentricities were not only not a barrier to acceptance, but in some circles, they were even prized. He developed a wicked sense of humor. He found boyfriends. He became a very good bridge player. He began collecting records. Bach was his favorite.

He graduated cum laude and applied to grad school. He had his heart set on the ivy league, especially Princeton, which was sufficiently close to the city and also still had the aura of F. Scott Fitzgerald and the bohemia of the nineteen twenties. But he had to "settle" (as he put it) for Columbia. He kept his Village walkup apartment and made the daily commute uptown where he pursued his Ph.D. in English literature specializing (of course) in the eighteenth century.

Timing in life as well as comedy is everything. At the end of Harrison's first year in graduate school his classmates who were graduating with their Ph.D.s sent out twenty or so job applications and typically received a dozen or more requests for transcripts and letters of recommendation, at least four or five requests for interviews, then later out of these they received two or three or sometimes more offers of employment which allowed room for negotiation and choice. Three years later when Harrison received his Ph. D. the market had changed radically. Harrison and all his other fellow graduates sent out hundreds of job applications and hoped and prayed they would get one offer. Many didn't. Harrison not only sent out three hundred fifty applications but for good measure joined an agency that promised to do its best to find him a job. All of these efforts came up empty until at the last minute, in the middle of August, the agency informed him that Sacred Heart, a small Catholic college in Wichita, Kansas, would like to interview him for the job of department head.

Department head? Kansas? Sacred Heart? He flew to Wichita and was picked up at the airport in a white van with "Sacred Heart" printed in red letters on the side. The driver was a middle aged man with a crew cut that had once been red but was now sprinkled with gray. The one other passenger was the president of the college, Sister Immaculata, who was wearing the very latest "modern" uniform of the American nun, a polyester suit with a metal cross around her neck, sensible shoes and a headpiece that showed at least half of her snow white hair. She had a distracted and harried air and a permanent smile. The driver, whose name was Carl proved to be one-third of the English department. When they arrived on campus, Harrison met the other two-thirds, a very obese ex-nun named Wendy Walters who seemed to be in a constant state of apology and a very elderly man with a neat mustache who was mostly silent.

Later, at a meal paid for by Carl at a local café, Harrison, after some discreet questions and then after a few beers, some more pointed questions, learned the facts of life about "The Heart" which is what everyone called the school. Here is what he learned: the school only had an enrollment of six hundred seventy-two students. As far as Harrison could tell, the place had no real reason to exist. Sister Immaculata was a sweetheart, but she had no earthly idea how she was going to keep the place afloat. Wendy was a terrible teacher, but she was so inept and neurotically needy (and she had tenure) that there was no real chance she would be fired. The very elderly man with the neat mustache was named Abel Shaw. Everyone called him A.B., supposedly because of his name, Abel, but really because he was an A.B.D., all but dissertation, from Kansas State. A new department head was being hired because A.B. suffered from narcolepsy, which meant that most of his classes lasted no more than ten minutes or so before he would nod off and the students would tiptoe out of the room, trying not to wake him. The new department head's first and most important task was to fabricate a good reason to fire him, which shouldn't be very hard, Carl assured Harrison, because there were dozens of complaints from co-eds that A.B. was not only a narcoleptic but also a notorious lech.

Carl himself had two masters degrees, one each from the University of Kansas and Kansas State. He was a confirmed bachelor, a daily communicant, the organist at St. Henry church, and his favorite activity was to sit up in his bed with a pitcher of martinis and a pile of freshman comp papers.

Harrison realized that life at "The Heart" would be unrelentingly awful. He also realized, however, that unemployment would be worse. Carl told him that the job would be his if he discreetly assured Sister Immaculata that he was willing to tackle the job of firing A.B. without any bad publicity for the school. Harrison agreed and ordered another beer.

Upon taking possession of his department head office, Harrison made the acquaintance of his secretary, an elderly lady named Mildred who seemed to have very few duties beyond manning the phone and endlessly crocheting. He closed the door of his office, pulled out a piece of paper with the Sacred Heart letter head and wrote on the top "Goal: Get Out of Here." Then he made a list of his plans.

Number one was to get rid of A.B. This proved to be much easier than he could have predicted. He requested and got the thick dossier of complaints and called A.B. into his office where he informed him that he had a deal for him that he was sure to like. Announce his retirement and Harrison would not pursue any prosecution of A.B. for the obvious violations of both university policies and the criminal code. Plus, he would give A.B. a nice retirement party. A.B. accepted and given the state of the job market, Harrison had no trouble finding a replacement for him immediately.

Next, he reviewed the job description of department head and after determining that a good deal of the administrative duties were purely clerical and mostly consisted of filling out and maintaining various forms, most of which served little or no purpose and were never actually used for anything, he spent a day instructing his secretary Mildred and made a short pamphlet describing in detail her new "duties."

Relieved of most of his extra work, he now declared that he was taking not one but two classes off his schedule because of the burden of being department head. He assigned all the freshmen and sophomore classes to Wendy and Carl and all the upper division classes to himself and his new hire, a woman with a doctorate from Notre Dame.

Having cleared his schedule of most of the more onerous tasks, Harrison now turned his attention to padding his curriculum vitae in view of his most pressing goal, escaping from the confines of the Heart. In this he was helped by the fact that Carl for years had been publishing something called the Kansas Triquarterly, a hodgepodge of execrable student stories and poems with occasional semi-scholarly work done by Carl and his friends. Harrison became Carl's friend and in short order published three essays with sufficiently scholarly titles that he hoped would pass muster with prospective employers who had never set eyes on the *Kansas Triquarterly.*

Next he set about writing some real scholarship and sending it off to more respectable journals and scholarly magazines. He recycled bits of his dissertation and papers he had written in grad school and sent them off. In due time they all came back with polite rejection slips. He recycled them for another round and once again they were rejected. He was proud of his dissertation and was sure there were at least two very good articles to be gleaned from its pages. No luck.

In a rage, he spent one weekend assembling an article that was filled with obfuscation, nonsense and exaggeration, peppered with every au courant critical word or phrase he could think of. He used "semiotic" and "deconstruction" liberally. He had many footnotes and he was careful to include quotations from Deridda and other icons. Several of the quotations were in German and French which he did not bother to translate. He sent it off to the most prestigious scholarly journal of English literature there is, the PMLA, and was rewarded by an acceptance with the caveat that he should rewrite section two, the only really clear and sensible part of the whole enterprise.

Armed with an acceptance from the PMLA he once again sent out slightly rewritten and newly titled versions of his earlier essays and in short order had two more publications. By the end of his second year at the Heart he had a respectable résumé and he began sending out letters of application to more congenial colleges written on his department letter head. He was sure to emphasize NYU and Columbia and to point out his scholarly output, particularly the PMLA. All this effort resulted in polite letters citing the market, the economy and their sincere hope that Harrison would find employment elsewhere. Harrison was forced to endure another year at the Heart.

As the end of Harrison's third academic year at the Heart drew to a close and he had still not succeeded in getting an offer from any other college, Harrison was growing desperate. He even consulted a counselor, a psychologist who told him he was suffering from depression, and recommended various books and exercises that he assured Harrison would be "helpful." "Do you mean melancholy?" Harrison asked, to which the counselor answered, "Well, that is not quite a clinically accepted term, but yes, melancholy is another way of putting it. Quaint but factual."

Harrison had always thought of himself as "quaint but factual" and so he went home and after rummaging a bit in the boxes of books he had never unpacked (a sign that he was only visiting here in Kansas, although the visit was now prolonged to three years), and there in the bottom of the third box he opened was what he was looking for: Robert Burton's eccentric masterpiece *The Anatomy of Melancholy*. He began to read.

The next day he was still reading. It was propped up on his desk at school when his secretary Mildred brought in the mail. Ads. Bills. Flyers. The usual. The usual. What's this? A letter from a university. Probably just another in a long line of rejections. But when he opened the envelope he was amazed to find that the first words after the greeting were not the usual "I am sorry to inform you", but the glorious words "I am pleased to let you know." A job offer! At last! At that moment the telephone rang.

Years later Harrison would reflect that while at the time the telephone message was decidedly bad news and while the interruption the telephone caused in his life also caused him to lose the job he had been offered, that all in all the timely or untimely telephone had saved him from transferring his life to a place that was probably only marginally better than the hell hole he had been occupying for three years.

On the phone was his father's sister, his Aunt Rose, who informed Harrison that his mother had died. Two weeks in Louisiana. The arrangements. The wake. The funeral. Aunt Rose helped, but his father was hopeless and helpless. At the end of two weeks, Harrison was actually eager to get back to Kansas. That's when he thought of the letter. A quick call to the university confirmed what he feared. The position had already been filled. "When we didn't hear from you...I am so sorry about your mother...I hope you are successful in your job search...Good luck."

Meanwhile, Harrison's father was mounting a campaign designed to convince Harrison that he should stay here at home. He was lost without his wife. Aren't there colleges here in New Orleans? Doesn't Tulane have an English department? Why don't you go down there and tell them you're available?

Harrison tried to inform his father about the realities of the job market but he wouldn't listen. "Would it kill you to just go on down there and ask?"

Finally, to satisfy his father, he agreed and on a hot, humid July afternoon he walked unannounced into the office of the head of the English department where he found a scene of chaos. The secretary had been crying. Various professors and students were milling around the door.

"Oh, it's just terrible," the secretary was saying. "One of our professors, Dr. Melvin, died very suddenly last night."

If you want to make God laugh, tell him your plans.

The professor who died was the one and only eighteenth century specialist in the department. Harrison was hired on the spot.

Scene Four: A Friendly Game of Cards

Ten years after that fateful day when Harrison walked into the English department office at Tulane, a math teacher named Paul Corman, a fellow member of the faculty senate, invited Harrison to join him and some other colleagues and friends for what he called "our weekly hump day poker game." Harrison had not played poker in years, but he was intrigued. In the years since resettling in New Orleans he had purchased a carriage house in the French Quarter and filled it with eighteenth century furniture and engravings. He already had a reputation as an eccentric and not only because he still dressed exclusively in three piece suits. He also smoked English oval cigarettes and drove an MG Midget, British racing green with tan leather interior. He also was the only conservative in the department, but was forgiven this anomaly because of his startlingly obscene sense of humor and his always entertaining attempts to bring sweet reason to bear in departmental meetings.

If only his colleagues could see him at home they would have been perhaps a bit more circumspect in their praise. Or maybe not. No one likes a good eccentric more than a college professor. At any rate, Harrison's home was comfortable and congenial and well appointed. Persian rugs. Eighteenth century engravings, bought one at a time at great expense. A considerable wine cabinet. Many, many books. But most salient of all was his bedroom dominated by a four poster bed complete with canopy and beside the bed a table. And on the table a marble ash tray meticulously clean. A bottle of very old and very expensive port. A crystal wine glass. In the drawer of the bedside table there were two receptacles: an old brown leather pouch full of a special blend of tobacco that included not only burly and Virginia but Louisiana's own perique and a wood inlaid box that contained nuggets of hashish. There also was an old bent briar pipe, dark with the stain of tobacco and the oils of Harrison's own skin where he rubbed the pipe on the side of his nose, and an even older yellowing meerschaum carved in the shape of an Indian head complete with feathers. There also was a Zippo lighter with the insignia of the United States Marine Corps, a gift from his father who had managed to live through Guam, Bougainvillea and Iwo Jima.

In the armoire whose mirrored doors reflected a Japanese print of a flowering cherry tree was a pair of deep forest green pajamas, a floor length black silk robe and a fez, Harrison's accustomed dress when he lay on his bed, propped up by down pillows, poured a glass of port, opened the bedside drawer, chose either briar and tobacco or meerschaum and hash, then reached for the thick book that was forever on his bed, the book with which he hoped to conquer the one flaw in what he thought of as not only a rational and civilized, but nearly perfect life. It was *The Anatomy of Melancholy*.

When Paul Corman asked Harrison if he would like to play a friendly game of cards, Harrison reflected that perhaps a weekly game of cards might be just what the doctor ordered.

"Poker," he said, "how droll. Yes. I would love to play some cards."

Scene Five: Gutter Punks #1

Harrison stood gazing at his face in his bathroom mirror. He was attempting to staunch the flow of blood from the long scratch that ran down his left cheek from just beside his ear almost to his jaw, but each time he applied a strip of toilet paper to his face, it came away red and the blood continued to flow. He was upset with this development, but what upset him even more was that the face that stared back at him, his own face, bore a striking resemblance to the face of his father.

Finally he wadded up several strips of the toilet paper and left them there hanging on his cheek. It was almost two in the morning. The boys had just left. He had been foolish to invite them in with a promise of hashish and a hope that they would be up for a well compensated roll in his canopy bed. For one thing there were two of them. For another, their appearance did not invite confidence. One was covered with tattoos and the other had a ridiculous blue Mohawk.

Usually Harrison was very careful and circumspect in choosing potential partners. He confined himself to one or the other of the well known gay bars, usually Yazoo on Bourbon Street. He preferred out of towners, tourists with their inhibitions down, who were, perhaps a little shy. The two gutter punks had charmed him with their broad hints that they were up for some "fun" and they had been very polite despite their garish appearance.

Harrison had been shocked, but in retrospect not really surprised when tattoo guy, once he had his hands on the hash, had slapped Harrison across the face. Tattoo guy had been surprised when his ring had opened up the gash on Harrison's cheek.

"Oh, sorry, man," he had said.

Mohawk guy had been more circumspect. "Let's get out of here. Come on, man. Let's go."

Harrison began to peel the toilet paper off his cheek. Better. It was better. He wet a wash cloth with cold water, dabbed at the small trickle of blood. It was almost stopped. His father's face continued to stare back at him not with concern but disapproval.

Scene Six: Gutter Punks #2

The next day was Wednesday, hump day, poker night. The other guys asked him what happened to his face.

"Shaving accident," Harrison said. Although the length and location made this claim unlikely, everyone politely decided to pretend to believe him. "OK," Harrison said, shuffling the cards, "Let's play a little Omaha."

The game went on with its usual ebbs and flows and when the last hand of showdown was dealt, Harrison was up seventy-two dollars. Timing, as everyone knows, is everything and if the game had lasted ten minutes more or less Harrison would have been home in his green silk pajamas, long black robe, fez and lying in his bed with his port, pipe and *The Anatomy of Melancholy* when the gutter punks came calling again and he could have kept them safely locked out. Or else they would have come and gone before he pulled up in his green MG. But there they were turning the corner on Decatur just as he was getting out his key.

They had a plan, but upon seeing Harrison on the deserted street, the plan left their heads and they pounced on him and after a thorough beating that included several kicks in the ribs they took his wallet and ran off toward Esplanade. For the second night in a row Harrison stood in his bathroom inspecting his face in the mirror. His nose was bloodied. His left eye was shut and bruised. His chest stabbed him with pain when he breathed in hard. Could there be a broken rib? He cleaned his face, got undressed, lay down on his bed. Out of sheer habit his hand reached for and opened the drawer of his bedside table, but he closed it again without reaching in, without choosing either comforting pipe or pouch or box. Again his hand reached out and took up the book that was always by his bed, his constant companion and his everlasting study. He opened it at random as he sometimes did to see what wisdom or comfort or entertainment or distraction he could glean by chance from its pages. What he read was this:

"And those men which have no other object of their love, than greatness, wealth, authority, &c, are rather feared than beloved; nec amant quemquam, nec amantus ab ullo: and how so ever borne with for a time, yet for their tyranny and oppression, griping, covetousness, currish hardness, folly, intemperance, imprudence, and such like vices, they are generally odious, abhorred of all, both God and man. Non uxor salvum te rult, mon filius, omnes Vicini oderunt—wife and children, friends, neighbours, all the world forsakes them, would feign be rid of them, and are compelled many times to lay violent hands on them, or else God's judgments overtake them: instead of graces, come furies."

Scene Seven: Urologist

Harrison had been playing poker every Wednesday night for ten years when he sat down with his urologist and got the news.

"Well," the doctor said, "there's bad news and good news. It is, in fact, cancer. Obviously that's the bad news part. The good news is that it seems to be very slow growing, something that is not all that unusual with the prostate. I've seen these many, many times and in the vast majority of cases the patient lives a very long life and ends up dying of something else altogether."

Harrison appeared but did not feel calm and composed. He cleared his throat, shifted his weight in the chair and suddenly became hyper aware of his hands and wondered what, if anything, he should do with them.

He scratched his nose and then returned the foreign object that his hand had become to the arm rest. Finally he realized that he had to say something.

"So," he said, "what's the plan?"

Scene Eight: The Sands of Iwo Jima

Not long after Harrison received his diagnosis his Aunt Rose informed him that she was no longer able to care for his father whose dementia had reached a point that now required twenty-four hour supervision. "We've got to make some decisions," she said and Harrison fresh from his own decision about his prostate to "wait and watch," told his Aunt Rose that he would investigate the availability and quality of nursing homes.

As dementia took over Harrison's father's mind and body he increasingly lost all interest or even recognized anything in the present world he occupied and was transported in his imagination and memory to a bloody beach in the South Pacific where he had been wounded by Japanese mortar fire.

After exhausting all the possibilities in the area, Harrison settled on a facility called Sunrise Village, which of course all the staff and many of the inhabitants sardonically called Sunset. It was big and well-appointed with different departments ranging from assisted living to what was euphemistically termed "the memory unit" which was where Harrison's father ended up.

Harrison had to admit that the facility was comfortable and the décor attractive. There was art and flowering plants. There were comfortable chairs, tables, couches, multiple televisions, many entertaining programs including bingo, exercise, music, movies, even gardening and yoga. Nothing, however, could be done about the principal and most obvious element of décor, the distracted and often absent people who sat dozing in wheel chairs or wandered aimlessly about the halls talking to themselves or to people who were no longer alive. Mr. Rubenstein was given to making inflammatory speeches in a loud voice. Mrs. Bienvenue spent most of her time seated in the sun room trying to breast feed a china faced doll that was missing most of her hair. Not even the big elderly golden retriever who spent his days dozing in the sun could cheer up the depressing atmosphere where these lost people were housed.

At first Harrison's father looked at him with anger and hurt for being abandoned here. Then he looked with confusion and fear and finally with no recognition at all. Harrison brought flowers and listened to the familiar stories.

"I was a mortar man. Did you know that?"

"Yes, Dad."

"My loader was killed, you know."

"Yes."

"I got hit too. Shrapnel. Still have some. Million dollar wound the corpsman said. You're going home, buddy."

Harrison had been raised Catholic and while he willingly went to Mass on Sunday, avoided meat on Friday, attended Catholic schools, was confirmed, observed all the holy days of obligation and even wore a miraculous medal and had a rosary in the top drawer of his desk, he early on began to question, then doubt, and finally abandoned first some and then most of Catholicism's dogmas. By the time he entered high school he considered himself "a pious agnostic." He continued, however, to go to church not only to avoid drama with his parents but also because he genuinely liked the liturgy and the beauty of the experience.

For eight years, all throughout undergraduate school at NYU and grad school at Columbia he gave up going to church altogether and never gave it a thought. His days at Sacred Heart College once again exposed him to Catholic culture and he found he had missed it. He began to question the certainty of his doubt. He began to attend Mass again and to confront God himself with his questions, an exercise that he sometimes found to be intriguing and infinitely absorbing and sometimes scared him to death.

Once he had purchased his French Quarter house he was within walking distance of St. Louis Cathedral and he not only attended Mass on Sunday but frequently on week days as well. In Harrison's well ordered life everything had its place: fresh squeezed juice, café au lait, cathedral visit, well planned classes, port, pipe and *The Anatomy of Melancholy* where one night he read these words:

"Nature binds all creatures to love their young ones; a hen to preserve her brood will rush upon a lion, a bird will fight with a bull, a sow with a bear, a silly sheep with a fox. So the same nature with a man to love his parents, (dii me pater omnes oderint, nit e magis quam oculos amen meos!) and this love cannot be dissolved, as Tully holds without detestable offence: but much more God's commandment, which enjoins a filial love, and an obedience in this kind."

Harrison looked up. "Oh Lord," he said. "Oh Lord, I don't even know if you're there, but if you are, please, please forgive me because I'm not at all sure I love my father."

As Harrison was reading these words his father was finally asleep dreaming, as usual, of the moment the shell fell behind him and his loader was killed and he himself felt the searing, burning pain in his back. Before falling asleep he had looked around the shadows of his room. "Where is this?" he asked himself. "Who are these people who come and go? Who is that man who keeps bringing flowers? Am I dead? Is this hell?"

Scene Nine: Surgery

The man who pushed the gurney toward the operating room was a black drag queen named Star. "Don't you worry, Dr. H." he said, "everything is going to be fine." Harrison was not so sure, but he was happy to hear the voice of Star anyway. He was very happy to hear that voice.

"Most of the time." "Usually." "The odds are good." That's what the urologist had said. "We'll wait and see. Keep an eye on it. You'll be fine. Really. I've seen this a thousand times. You'll be fine." But most of the time is not all of the time. Odds are good is not the same as a sure thing. Harrison knew that from playing poker. "You know what this is, doc?" he had asked. "It's a bad beat. That's what it is."

The doctor, who was also a poker player, knew what he meant. "Well then," he said, "time to go all in."

Scene Ten: Last Hand

There were side effects from the surgery and even more side effects from the chemo and the other meds. Harrison lost his desire but he kept his desire to desire. He also lost forty-five pounds and all his hair. He took a leave from the university and also from his weekly poker game. Two months later there was more bad news. The cancer had spread.

He was not yet bed ridden but he was always tired and the days stretched out in front of him without relief or even variety. What to do? How fill up the time? He took short walks, stopping in frequently at St. Louis Cathedral to continue his argument with God, a mid afternoon café au lait at the Café du Monde. Sitting on the moonwalk and watching the river traffic. It wasn't enough.

Harrison had been very happy with his life. He loved his teaching, his research, the camaraderie of academia, even his poker game. His house was his refuge. It was filled with beauty and comfort, art and culture, all the accoutrements of what Harrison thought were the trappings not only of civilization but the good life. Now all that, all of it, seemed to Harrison to have changed suddenly, very suddenly into meaningless displays, empty, doomed. "If I'm going to die," Harrison thought, "if I'm going to die...."

He began to wonder, "what have I left undone? What can I do now to fill up the time I have left? What can I do that I haven't done yet?"

The obvious answer was to once and for all settle his debate with God, but Harrison could not imagine how in the world he was to accomplish this. Instead he decided to have a poker party.

A poker party might seem like an odd choice, but to Harrison it made perfect sense. Lying in bed with *The Anatomy of Melancholy* or lying on the couch in the living room listening to Bach he came to realize that while he had many acquaintances and colleagues he did not really have any friends, not what you could really call a friend. He got along well with his fellow teachers, his neighbors and his poker playing regulars, but never, not even once had he been inside any of their houses and not one of them had ever been inside his. There was no one he could think of that he could call, suggest a visit, certainly no one who would think to visit him on their own. He began to make plans.

There were six other regular card players in the hump day poker game. He would invite them all to his house for a nice meal and then a friendly game of cards. He spent a pleasant afternoon planning the party, making a list of groceries he would need, the menu. A ham. Paté. Maybe some nice smoked salmon. A big pot of gumbo. A fresh fruit salad. A cake. A big cake. Coconut. That would be nice. He called all the regulars: Tommy, Paul, Cap, the Chief of campus police, the Chef, head of campus food services, and the coach of the baseball team. Tommy, the owner of the sandwich shop where the regular game took place, gave Harrison a definite maybe as did Paul, a professor in the math department. Cap said yes. Coach and Chief said no. With only Cap a definite yes, Harrison told the Chef to bring his new bride and then for good measure he invited his Aunt Rose.

The night of the party his sideboard was full of enough food to feed fifty people. Cap came early and then Aunt Rose. The only other poker regular to come was the Chef and his new wife, Annette. Everyone praised Harrison for the wonderful food, but it was obvious that the party was a bust. There were only five people for the poker game and two of them, Annette and Aunt Rose, were not really poker players. After they all had their pieces of coconut cake, Cap tried to put on a brave face and told Harrison, "I don't know about you, but I'm ready for some cards." He began to shuffle the deck. The chef made a cheat sheet on a napkin for Annette, a list of poker hands. They began to play.

Harrison tried to pretend that all was well, but he was feeling nauseous, wondered if perhaps he had a fever and below these physical complaints he was filled with what he recognized as embarrassment and shame. When he looked at the sideboard still full of food he realized that he was a fool.

Aunt Rose, knowing nothing about how to play poker, stayed in every hand and quickly lost the money that Harrison had given her. He bought her in again and again she quickly lost it all and declared it was time to go home. Everyone else took the opportunity to express concern for Harrison who was not looking well and Harrison did not protest when they all made ready to leave.

After they were gone, Harrison began to put away all the food, but he was overcome with a wave of nausea and had to sit on his kitchen stool until it passed. As he sat there with his head on the counter there was a knock on the door. He tried to stand but had to sit again. Finally he went to the door and saw that the Chef and Annette were outside. When he opened the door Chef said, "Annette told me we were rude not to offer to help you clean up." Annette touched Harrison's arm. "Are you all right?" she asked.

He wasn't. They took him to the living room and made him lie down. "You stay here with Harrison," Annette said. "I'll put away the food."

"I'm OK," Harrison said.

"No you're not, buddy," the Chef said, "You just relax."

"It wasn't much of a party, was it?" Harrison asked.

The Chef laughed. "Well, the food was great. The cards, not so much."

After Annette cleaned up, they put Harrison to bed and told him they'd check on him tomorrow. Harrison did not pour a glass of port. He did not open the drawer and select a pipe. He didn't even open *The Anatomy of Melancholy*. He tried to sleep, but not long after he had dozed off he was swept by a wave of nausea and just made it to the bathroom before kneeling down on the tile floor and emptying his stomach into the toilet. He stayed on the floor for awhile and then got up unsteadily and looked without pity into the bathroom mirror before opening the cabinet and getting out the sleeping pills his doctor had prescribed. He took one. Then he took another one. After the second one, it was easier to take some more and finally the whole bottle. "What the hell," he said, and lay down on his bed.

Scene Eleven: Whatever Satisfies

Harrison did not believe in luck. Since he was a student and a firm believer in eighteenth century rationalism he felt sure that reality was governed by laws that could be discovered and understood if only we knew enough facts and applied sweet reason in appropriate measures. All of his years of poker playing reinforced this belief. He was not himself the best poker player in his group, but he could easily see how inevitable and immutable the laws of probability played out in the game and how the best players relied not on luck but on skill and knowledge to pull in winning pots.

Life, of course, is complicated and sometimes he was tempted by doubts and even fears that reality might be just chaos, but these were fleeting temptations and he recognized them as such. They were merely the remnants of emotions and frustrations that rushed in to supply bogus explanations when knowledge was incomplete. He resisted their siren song and remained convinced that despite the obvious chaos he saw everywhere there was after all and ultimately a rational explanation for everything.

It was Dr. Schlosser who had convinced him. Dr. Schlosser was his favorite professor at Columbia. There were many dynamic and charismatic teachers in the English department and even a couple who might be described as gurus. Dr. Schlosser was not one of these. He was decidedly old school and he looked the part of the clichéd college professor, wearing tweed jackets with leather elbow patches. He even smoked a pipe. He had a neat and trimmed mustache, unruly hair, broad old fashioned ties. He never used class notes, rarely asked questions or encouraged discussions. He gave lectures and his lectures were not easy to comprehend or to summarize. They were delivered in not only complete but eloquent sentences, but never gave the impression that they were memorized or rehearsed.

It was impossible to take notes. You were forced to listen. Most students didn't like him much and he did nothing to encourage friendship. Harrison thought he was great.

Early on in the semester of the first class Harrison took from Dr. Schlosser, a course in eighteenth century non-fiction prose, Dr. Schlosser gave a lecture that changed Harrison's life. Later Harrison himself would replicate the lecture in his own classroom and he came to see it as the foundation of everything he liked about his chosen specialty and even the foundation of what Harrison thought of as his "philosophy of life."

Here is what Dr. Schlosser and later Harrison told their students:

"Today we are going to learn something very important. In fact, it is the most important thing you are going to learn this semester. Perhaps it is the most important thing you will ever learn. Don't take notes. Just listen.

"First a fact: in parts of the world where the temperature at least sometimes falls below thirty-two degrees, bodies of water freeze. Lakes, ponds, rivers, even the ocean will turn to ice. But the water does not freeze all the way down. In even the coldest climates there is always free flowing liquid water under the ice. This is a fact.

"Now, I am going to make two statements about this fact and I want you to tell me which of these two statements makes the most sense. Ready? OK. Statement number one: Fish are able to live because the water does not freeze all the way down. Statement number two: The water does not freeze all the way down so the fish can live."

In both Dr. Schlosser's class and later in Harrison's the smarter students would sometimes laugh. In any case, a quick show of hands always indicated that all (or almost all) the students thought the first statement made sense and the second statement was silly.

"Good," Dr. Schlosser (and later Harrison) would say, "You are good modern people. Most people alive today would agree with you. In fact, most people since the seventeenth century would agree with you. But guess what? Prior to the seventeenth century most people—even very smart people like yourselves would have chosen the second statement as the most sensible. Why?

"I'll tell you why. Because when smart people prior to the seventeenth century wanted to investigate some part of the world, some part of reality and to understand it, the question they asked was "Why?" Why is something the way it is? In other words they wanted to know its *purpose*, its *goal*. Now most of these people—these very smart people, mind you—knew perfectly well what the *general* answer to the question was. Why is something the way it is? Because God wants it that way. God has a plan. He has a purpose. So why does the water only freeze part of the way down? Clearly it is so the fish can live.

"But all that changed in the seventeenth century. Some smart people began to ask a different question. They started to ask the question "how?" Perhaps they got tired of asking why. Perhaps they began to doubt that God, if He existed at all, had a plan. Who knows? At any rate the answer to the question why no longer satisfied them. They wanted to know how.

"This change began in the seventeenth century but it finally triumphed in the eighteenth, an age now forever known as the Age of Reason. Prior to then, all the answers to why had just sat there doing nothing whatever. Oh, they satisfied, but they did not result in anything like an increase in knowledge. But once people asked how all hell broke loose. The world changed. For a thousand years the plow used by farmers had remained exactly the same. The horse had been the principal means of transportation. But once people asked how—science was born –and technology—and before you knew it the industrial revolution. Steam power. Railroads. The internal combustion engine. Cars. Planes. Jets. Rockets. Electricity. Nuclear power. Computers. The modern world. Why? Who knows? How? Hey, we can do that.

"So what is a good explanation? It is an explanation that *satisfies*. Once upon a time the satisfying answer was the answer to the question why. No more. Now we are only satisfied by the explanation of how.

"Many things have happened in the history of mankind but there have only been a few truly transformative ideas. This is one of them and if you hope to understand the modern world or even understand eighteenth century literature, you must understand this revolution in the way people think. I don't know much, but I do know this: I can ask how and if I have enough facts and enough brain power I can get a satisfying answer. But I can ask why from now until doomsday and I'll never be satisfied."

Harrison was always pleased with this lecture. The students got it. It was profound. It was easy to reference over and over again throughout the semester. "What is a good explanation?" Harrison would ask and the students would dutifully reply, "Whatever satisfies." "Good," Harrison would say, but deep in his heart Harrison had a secret. As much as he wanted to believe that reason, sweet reason, especially as practiced in the eighteenth century, was an unassailable philosophy, a philosophy to live by, deep, deep in Harrison's heart he was not satisfied. He had to admit that to him the second statement answered the question that he really wanted to know. Why? he asked.

Why was what he asked the silent God in St. Louis Cathedral. Why was what he asked himself. He knew the how of cancer cells. So what? That didn't satisfy. He could tell you what he should have done to assure himself he didn't die alone, but he wanted more. He wanted to know why. He knew the way of all flesh and he was sure someone was working even now to explain the hour of mortality and the inevitable death of cells. But why?

On his last night on earth he knew perfectly well how his medications had caused his nausea, caused him to kneel in front of the toilet and lose the remnants of the food he had so carefully prepared for his party. He knew the hour of aging and so as he stared at his face in the bathroom mirror he was not surprised by what he saw. He even knew the how of melancholy not only from his relentless reading of his old friend and adversary, the book that was always at hand, but from professionals and counselors who had applied their expertise to his problem over the years. He even knew why his party was such a bust. None of this was a mystery to him. What was a mystery was why he should go on living.

Harrison was an intelligent and a learned man, but when he asked why, he felt like a naïve and ignorant and even annoying child. There was no hope of a satisfying answer and no relief from asking the question. Even as the pills he took on his final night sent him deeper into and then out of himself, sick as he was, he was still crying, begging to know from what he hoped was a merciful God, the answer to the question that would satisfy. "Oh Lord," he said, "hold me. Hold me, hold me, hold me. Whisper to me. Soft. Let me know. Why? Why, why, why?"

OLD WAR WOUNDS

Mr. Simoneaux loved his son. He loved his daughter-in-law and he loved their two little boys, his only grandchildren. He did not, however, love living with them, even if it was supposedly only temporary. His son had said, "Dad, while you're doing the chemo, come stay with us. You can go back home when it's over."

Mr. Simoneaux was grateful but skeptical about that "when" it's over. He knew his son meant "if" not "when" but hey, hope is good. Hope is a good thing. There's always hope. Except, of course, when there isn't. So now he was on the north shore in his son's home in St. Tammany Parish awaiting another dozen chemo treatments and depending on how they went, maybe some radiation. And depending on how that went, well...he didn't like to contemplate what then. His home in New Orleans was only forty miles away. It might as well have been a thousand.

It was October 28, three days before Halloween, when Mr. Simoneaux moved into his son's spare bedroom. When the car pulled into the driveway Mr. Simoneaux saw that his son—or more likely his daughter-in-law—had gone all out in decorating the house for the holiday. There was a cardboard witch on the front door and two cardboard skeletons hung from the porch. In the front lawn there was a scarecrow with a Frankenstein mask and a jack-o-lantern was on the front steps. Inside the house his grandsons barely paused to say hello and give him hugs because their mother was fitting them out in their new homemade costumes. Joel, the six year old, was a panda bear and Harrison, the three year old, was dressed as a tiger. Mr. Simoneaux took pictures and they all had donuts and cider even though it was only an hour until supper.

After supper and baths Mr. Simoneaux told Joel and Harrison stories of his own trick or treating days. "In my day, kids went out alone," he said. "And we played tricks on people."

"What kind of tricks, Grandpa?"

"Be careful, Dad, don't give them any ideas," his son said.

After the kids were in bed they all had a lot of laughs over the way Halloween had changed.

"I can't believe you and Mom let me go out trick or treating alone," his son said.

"We'd never let Joel and Harrison do that," his daughter-in-law said.

"It's a new world," Mr. Simoneaux said.

"Did you hear about the Reverend Beckham?" his son asked.

It seems their neighbor, two doors down, was pastor of some holy-roller church that thought Halloween was pagan and trick or treating should be banned. He even sent a delegation to the city council. Nothing came of it, of course, and the city council officially set trick or treating for 6-8 p.m. on October 30.

"Why October 30?" Mr. Simoneaux wanted to know. "Why fool with the calendar? Halloween is Halloween." His son shrugged. "LSU game is Saturday night. Maybe that's why," he said.

The night of October 30 it was still light when his son and daughter-in-law took their little panda bear and tiger trick or treating in the neighborhood. Along with all the other vigilant parents they held firmly onto their offspring's hands, and instructed them to say

Thank You and *Happy Halloween*, while getting their rations of suckers and Tootsie Rolls and mini Snickers and Milky Ways. Mr. Simoneaux stayed at home on the front porch manning the candy bowl and sipping hot cider.

At first there was a rush of children with the adults holding back on the sidewalk and the kids eagerly opening their bags for the handfuls of goodies and then there was a trickle and then little more than an hour after it started, it was over. Porch lights stayed on awhile more but since almost all the kids out trick or treating were pre-school and early grade school, their parents already had them home, their bags inspected and their pjs on. The porch lights began to blink off. Kids were tucked in and parents poured wine and cider and began to think about Thanksgiving.

The next day Mr. Simoneaux tagged along with his daughter-in-law and the boys to the playground in the park. He loved his grandsons and he genuinely enjoyed playing with them, even getting down on the floor or in the dirt, but he had a time limit and they didn't. Long after Mr. Simoneaux was tired and bored and longed for a little peace, they would still be going strong and demanding his attention. The playground meant swings to push and slides that demanded close attention when Harrison climbed up the ladder.

Luckily there was another young mother with two boys of her own and the four kids went to play in the sand pile while the women talked. Mr. Simoneaux sat in the sun and idly watched and half listened to the women as they exchanged notes on babysitters and diets and yoga classes.

As he half dozed on the bench he heard a kid call out "Grandpa!" He opened his eyes to see a tall white haired man walking down the path toward the playground. The man carried an oxygen unit on his shoulder and had a tube attached to his nose. Despite this encumbrance his walk was steady and his bearing was erect. He was probably a good ten or even twenty years older than Mr. Simoneaux but he had the look of an athlete or maybe a soldier. He had thick white hair, a luxurious white mustache neatly trimmed, straight back, a good set of teeth.

The women had moved over to the sandbox and he could see that they were talking about him. The other grandpa glanced over toward him and Mr. Simoneaux could imagine that they had told him something along the lines of "Why don't you go on over there and talk to that other old codger." In a moment he was moving toward Mr. Simoneaux's bench and holding out his hand.

There are two kinds of World War II veterans. There are those who never talk about their experiences at all and there are those who rarely talk about anything else. Arthur Grooms was a member of the latter group. It was clear he had a world of stories and was always on the lookout for a brand new audience. Mr. Simoneaux barely got in a word for half an hour.

It seems Arthur Grooms had been a frogman in the Navy. He had a lot of bitter words for all the glory the army took for D-Day and asked pointedly if Mr. Simoneaux knew who were the first people to hit the beaches? And, of course, it turns out it was the frogmen. It also turned out that Arthur Grooms was one of them. There was a lot of description, a lot of acronyms, confusing letters and slang as well as words like "ordnance" and the casual phrase, "the first time I was shot." Mr. Simoneaux only had time to nod his head or say "My" or "What do you know?" before Mr. Grooms was off on another chilling adventure, humorous anecdote, interesting detail.

Mr. Grooms was a career navy man. He was one of the first Navy Seals, helped to organize the unit, was battlefield commissioned, saw action in Korea, was one of the principal instructors in the Navy Seal school, complained bitterly about how the Navy stuck him on a desk, hinted broadly of top secret doings in Haiphong Harbor in Vietnam, his own top secret, highest echelon involvement with Delta Force, a long disquisition on military medicine and its shortcomings that followed the phrase, "the last time I was shot."

Eventually—as was inevitable—the conversation turned to medicine and their various ailments and here Mr. Simoneaux was able to trump Arthur's little case of emphysema with his own cancer and chemo before Arthur wrested superiority again with a couple grisly tales of his old war wounds and his own wife's death a decade before in a car accident.

They were both going strong with tales of their grandchildren's extraordinary exploits when Mr. Simoneaux's daughter-in-law returned and herded her reluctant boys—Harrison crying much to Mr. Simoneaux's embarrassment—into the van and then home where Mr. Simoneaux could make himself a cup of tea and take a nap.

As he lay in his recliner in blessed solitary peace and sipped his tea and began to half doze he imagined himself swimming to the coastal barriers on the Normandy beaches, setting the ordnances in the pre-dawn, watching the horizon fill with ships, the thunder of the big naval barrages, the appearance of an armada of landing boats, the sky filled with smoke.

Mr. Simoneaux did not really regret having never been in the armed services. He came of age during Vietnam and he considered that war a colossal mistake and a huge waste and he did everything he could to avoid going. Luckily he managed to stay free of the draft through a combination of student deferments and a lucky lottery number. Still. Every man wonders if not wishes to really know what war would be like, how he would perform. But then would he have become an old bore like Arthur constantly retelling (and no doubt embellishing) his adventures? Mr. Simoneaux dreamed, drifting up and down in a doze, seeing himself in all the uniforms of all the services, running through a city street as an Army grunt, hitting the beach as a Marine, manning a big gun on a Navy ship, leather jacketed in a B-24 bombing run over Germany, even steering a landing ship as a Coast Guardsman. He didn't really want to do any of those things, but it would be nice to *have* done them, been a part of his past, his memories, his story.

After supper while he helped his daughter-in-law with the dishes and his son got the kids ready for bed, the doorbell rang and he went to answer it. It was already dark outside and it was very unusual for the doorbell to ring at this late hour, so he turned on the porch light and looked out through the window. There were two black boys, maybe fourteen or fifteen years old. One was wearing a floppy fedora and gripping a big rubber cigar in his teeth. The other was wearing a red cape and a Spiderman t-shirt. Hmm. Costumes?

He opened the door and the boys mumbled "Trick or Treat" and held out almost empty grocery bags.

"Trick or Treat was last night, boys," Mr. Simoneaux said.

"Yeah, we know," Spiderman said, "we couldn't go out last night."

"Hmm. Well, I think I may have something. Wait here."

"Who is it, Dad?" his son called from the bathroom where he was bathing the boys.

"Some trick or treaters."

"Trick or treaters? That was last night."

"Yeah, well." Mr. Simoneaux found the candy stash in the kitchen. His daughter-in-law looked up from the sink, "What is it?"

"Trick or treaters."

"Really?"

"Yeah. I got it covered."

"OK."

Mr. Simoneaux pulled the bag of candy out of the cupboard and walked to the porch.

"Here you go, boys," he said and dumped two big handfuls into each of the bags.

"Thanks."

"Thanks."

"Happy Halloween," Mr. Simoneaux said and closed the door.

Twenty minutes later the dishes were done and the boys were sitting on their Dad's lap as he read them for the thousandth time "Ten Little Monkeys." The doorbell rang again. Mr. Simoneaux was deep into a book, a mystery that was just about to get solved and he looked up annoyed.

"I'll get it," the daughter-in-law said.

"Put the porch light on," the son said.

"Want me to come?" Mr. Simoneaux said.

"I got it."

A moment later voices were raised and they heard the Reverend Beckham in full voice threatening to call the police.

"What in the world?" the son said. He and Mr. Simoneaux went to the porch to find the two black boys who had come earlier and behind them the Reverend Beckham who was waving around a small pistol and making threats.

"Jesus, Billy, put down that stupid gun," the son said.

"Do you know these boys?" the Reverend asked.

"I do," Mr. Simoneaux said, "They're trick or treating."

"Well, trick or treating was last night, not tonight."

"That's hardly a reason for a gun," the daughter-in-law said.

"These boys are way too old anyway."

"Put down the damned gun, Billy."

"Do you know what they were doing?"

"No."

"They were hiding in the bushes."

"Were you running around waving a gun? Cause if you were running around waving a gun, let me tell you, I'd be hiding in the bushes too."

"I just wanted to know…"

"We wasn't doin' nothin', Mister."

"They said they were here earlier."

"That's right."

"These are the trick or treaters?"

"Yes."

"Just let us go, Mister."

"I think we should call the police."

"Whatever for?"

"Or call their parents."

"Billy, go home. And put that stupid gun away. We'll take care of these boys."

"This is what comes of celebrating the devil's holiday. I told you. I told you, didn't I? I don't know how you can call yourself a Christian and have this godless jack-o-lantern out here on the steps."

"Billy," the son said, "what you need to do is to lighten up."

"Oh sure...."

And so it went for another five minutes. The black boys were silent, patiently waiting to see what would happen. Joel and Harrison were jumping up and down yelling "Trick or Treat." The four adults were trying as hard as they could to bring reason and logic to the discussion, but were all talking at the same time, convinced all would be well if the other three would just shut up. Finally, the Reverend left, throwing a few Bible verses back over his shoulder and warning that the city council would hear about this.

"Well, boys," Mr. Simoneaux's son said, once the Reverend was half way to his own house, "What do you want to do?"

"We want to go home," Spiderman said.

"You think we should call your parents?" the daughter-in-law asked.

"Oh Lord, no, don't do that. We'll be all right."

"Where do you live anyway?" Mr. Simoneaux asked. There were no black families in their subdivision.

"Over there." said the fedora wearer, waving vaguely to the east.

"Were you boys playing tricks on Mr. Beckham?"

"Oh no, sir," said Spiderman, "We were just going up the steps to trick or treat and this dog started barking and the lights came on and here was this man with a gun in his hand and we took off running and he was yelling and we hid behind those big bushes."

It seemed like a plausible story. Still.

"OK. Get on home," the son said. "And next year pay attention to the night that's supposed to be for trick or treating."

"Go straight home," the daughter-in-law said.

"Oh, yes, ma'am."

"We goin' straight home."

Mr. Simoneaux finished his mystery and started up a new one, but by nine o'clock it was clear that this one wasn't as good as the previous book and he abandoned it and said he was going to go back into his room and watch a little TV. His son and daughter-in-law were making elaborate shows of being tired, which Mr. Simoneaux knew meant they were planning on some love making and would soon retreat to their own bedroom.

There wasn't much on television. He tried reading awhile longer, sneaked out into the kitchen for some ice cream, tried the TV again and then at ten o'clock walked out into the back yard to look at the stars. As soon as he silently shut the door behind him he heard a noise, a kind of shuffling and then a snap and a scrape coming from the garage and what might be a voice and a whispered shush. Cautiously he walked to the side of the garage and listened. Yes, there were voices. He couldn't make out what they were saying. He got down on his hands and knees and feeling like an infantry man—or maybe one of Arthur Groom's Navy Seals—he crawled to the corner of the garage, lay flat on the ground and pulled himself forward enough to look around the corner into the garage itself. There were the two black boys. The one in the fedora was sitting on Joel's bike. Spiderman was rummaging through the freezer section of their extra refrigerator, stuffing popsicles and ice cream sandwiches into his trick or treat bag. Mr. Simoneaux wished he had a weapon. He even wished he had the Reverend's pistol. He would stand up, have them covered, trapped in the garage, ungrateful little bastards, and then he'd call the police. Then he heard them talking.

Spiderman turned around and held up a prize. "Look here. Drumsticks."

"Oooh, I love those drumsticks. Gimme one."

And they set to eating the ice cream treats. Suddenly they didn't seem like criminals. They seemed like kids, kids like he had been. He could imagine himself stealing ice cream on a Halloween night. Of course, he wouldn't steal a bike. But was the kid planning on stealing that bike? It sure looked like it.

"These are good."

"They got creamsicles too."

Mr. Simoneaux stood up.

"Hello, boys."

They froze.

"Shit!" said Spiderman.

"We ain't doin' nothin," said fedora man, quickly getting off the bike.

"So tell me, boys, tell me why I shouldn't call your mama—or the police."

Mr. Simoneaux had to shut them up; the whining, the self-defenses, the groveling, the obvious lies were just too depressing. He was beginning to dislike them again. A dog barked. It reminded Mr. Simoneaux of the Reverend's basset hound, a deep phlegmatic baritone. And that reminded Mr. Simoneaux of the Reverend himself. He had a vision of the ridiculous Reverend and his ridiculous rantings and his ridiculous gun and Mr. Simoneaux had an inspiration.

"Boys," he said, "I have an idea."

As he outlined his plan to the boys he felt like he was sure Arthur Grooms must have felt when he told his huddled Navy Seals their orders, spreading out the maps, distributing the equipment, double checking the ordnance. The boys were silent and unenthusiastic. Mr. Simoneaux was afraid they would run but no, they figured that putting up with this crazy white man and his plans was better than either going to jail or answering to their mamas so they sullenly listened and then even more sullenly obeyed his orders.

"OK," Mr. Simoneaux said, kneeling down in the garage. "Let's synchronize our watches."

"What's that now?" asked fedora guy.

"It's twenty-two hundred hours now. Let's see—twenty-two eighteen."

"What's that mean?" asked Spiderman.

"Well, in the military, after noon, they don't start over with one o'clock, they keep going. One o'clock is thirteen, two o'clock is fourteen and so on up to twenty-four hundred hours at midnight."

"That crazy."

"No, no, it's logical. Look...."

"Anyway, we don't have any watches."

"You don't?"

"No."

"Well, never mind. Look, here's a map of the Beckham house." And he began to draw in the dust on the garage floor.

"Why you drawing? We can see the house from here."

"Just pay attention. We have to plan this campaign. We don't want anything to go wrong."

Mr. Simoneaux told them his plan. As he gave his orders in quick, clipped sentences he felt adrenaline rising in his body. The smell of burning leaves was in the air and he imagined it was the smoke of battle. In his mind he heard the rattle of machine gun fire, the explosion of artillery shells. The shadows all around him held fighting men, friends and foe. Everyone was counting on him and his men to accomplish their mission. "Keep your heads down," he told the boys. " I don't want any casualties."

The boys nodded solemnly.

"Everyone clear on the plan?"

They nodded again.

"OK. Saddle up. Let's move out."

Carefully and silently they removed the Halloween decorations from the house: the two skeletons on the porch columns, the cardboard witch on the door, the real jack-o-lantern, and Mr. Simoneaux's favorite, the stuffed scarecrow with the Frankenstein mask seated on the leaf filled orange bag painted to look like a jack-o-lantern.

They brought all these things to a rendezvous point on the corner behind the azalea bush of the Reverend Beckham's house. Mr. Simoneaux knelt and gave his instructions. He handed out the duct tape he had secured from the garage. The boys were to go silently to the Reverend's porch and attach the skeletons and witch to the door and two front windows. Meanwhile, Mr. Simoneaux would assemble the Frankenstein scarecrow in the middle of their front walk and then return to place the jack-o-lantern on their front steps. Finally he would light the candle in the jack-o-lantern, they would ring the doorbell and then run like hell for the safety of the bushes across the street and have a good laugh on the Reverend when he came out to investigate and discovered his house desecrated by all these godless decorations. The boys didn't see the fun in all this, but they cheered up when Mr. Simoneaux found a particularly large pile of dog poop and decided to up the ante by putting it into one of the boy's paper bags and setting it on fire on the porch. He explained to the boys that the Reverend was sure to try to put it out by stomping on it and then—ha-ha!—he'd step into all the dog poop. The boys were a bit skeptical this would work, but thought it was worth trying anyway.

They argued a bit over which one of them would sacrifice his paper bag, but Mr. Simoneaux smoothed that out and then with a glance at his watch and a full three hundred sixty degree reconnaissance to make sure there weren't any bogeys out there—or barking dogs—he put a finger to his lip and then swung his arm toward the Reverend's house and sent them off on their silent mission.

They were perfect, slapping up the witch and skeletons. Meanwhile Mr. Simoneaux dragged the bag of leaves with one hand and awkwardly shouldered the Frankenstein scarecrow, steadily losing straw, with the other. It took longer than he had planned to get the scarecrow to remain upright and he was fumbling with the matches for the jack-o-lantern when he heard the dog bark.

"Here," he told Spiderman, tossing him the matches, "Light the poop."

Spiderman lit the poop and at that exact moment the porch light went on. The boys ran, not toward the bushes across the street, but away to the east, down the street and presumably toward home. Mr. Simoneaux froze, jack-o-lantern in his arm, kneeling on the front walk as the Reverend emerged from the house brandishing his gun.

Mr. Simoneaux's adrenaline level was at an all-time peak. It seemed to him that the Reverend, standing there in his blue striped pjs and waving the little pistol, was just the vanguard of a mighty force of know-nothing fascist yahoos intent on destroying all that was good and beautiful in the world. Mr. Simoneaux longed for a weapon. If he had one, he was sure he would use it, send that smug, self-righteous bastard falling backward through the open door, a gaping sucking wound in his chest, arms flailing impotently pulling down the cardboard witch on his front door as he hit the deck.

But Mr. Simoneaux had no weapon and he only had the satisfaction of seeing the Reverend stomping on the dog-shit bag and then he heard the little pop pop pop of his pistol and the jack-o-lantern in Mr. Simoneaux's arms exploded and at the same instant he felt a burning thump in his chest and with a combination of ecstasy and terror he realized "I've been shot."

The boys were gone. Mr. Simoneaux felt first a bitter disappointment that his troops had run, but then relief that they were safe and well out of it and he didn't have to worry about them or even account for their presence. This relief lasted only a second before he realized with horror that the Reverend was hopping about on the front porch pulling off his pj bottoms which were now on fire. Behind him the cardboard witch was also burning on his front door and the Reverend was yelling inside the door for his wife to bring water. Oh, thought Mr. Simoneaux, this is just about perfect. I carried out my mission. My men are safe. The enemy may not be dead, but he sure looks ridiculous. And here I am wounded. Hey, it's a good day to die. And a gunshot wound? So much better than stupid cancer. But then a fear rose in him, the most basic, most fundamental fear, and a desire, the most basic and fundamental desire and he knew that here, sitting on this suburban lawn with an exploded jack-o-lantern in his lap, he looked and felt every bit as ridiculous as the Reverend who by now was standing naked on the porch, leaning against one of the skeletons on his window and inspecting his left foot. No, all in all, Mr. Simoneaux decided, he wanted to live. All around him in the neighborhood people were cautiously coming out of their houses to survey the battle. There was the sound of a siren.

Police. Fire department. Ambulances. Two ambulances, one for Mr. Simoneaux and one for the Reverend who in addition to minor burns to his left leg had managed to accidentally shoot himself in the foot. Neighbors all roaming around in little groups mostly laughing. The fire ruined the front door and some of the porch paint but nothing else. Later he claimed more damage to the paint from the duct tape.

The emergency room doctor was amazed at Mr. Simoneaux's luck. The bullet—lucky for him only a .22—whizzed through his chest and managed to miss absolutely everything—heart, lungs, aorta, vertebral column, major arteries and came to rest just under the skin beside his right scapula. They made a small incision, popped it out, put on a bandage and he was good as new.

Mr. Simoneaux's son was at first completely puzzled and then as the facts came to-gether very angry at his father and then finally could not help but see the humor in the whole thing and couldn't stop laughing. Mr. Simoneaux's daughter-in-law brought him books and Halloween candy and homemade chicken soup in the hospital as if he were set for a long stay, but the next day he was home, feeling very embarrassed about the whole thing.

His son headed off a lawsuit and criminal charges, but was still responsible for quite a lot of money, which Mr. Simoneaux promised to repay but they both knew that was impossible.

The neighbors all pretty much disliked the Reverend, not so much for his religious beliefs which they didn't really care about, but because his stupid basset hound had a habit of shitting on other people's lawns. They made Mr. Simoneaux a hero and took to calling him Captain Midnight and then just Captain and sometimes Cap.

Two weeks later there was an article in the paper about a crew of little black boys who had been responsible for a whole string of garage burglaries mostly involving bikes. Mr. Simoneaux wasn't sure, but he thought he recognized two of the pictures as Spiderman and fedora guy.

He showed the picture to his son, but his son just shrugged. "Could be," he said, "hard to tell. Does it matter?"

"Well, I like to think they are good boys, just playing Halloween tricks. I don't like to think of them as thieves."

"Dad, do you ever…you know…regret…?"

"Hell, son, how can I not regret?"

"Yeah. Well, I just wondered…."

"So what do you regret, son?"

His son stood deciding. Then he sat down. His father waited as good fathers do and then he thought. "Oh Lord, if I could choose, I'd rather face enemy fire in the surf or a rice paddy than be here right now." But, of course, he didn't have a choice. This was his war and he was determined to behave honorably.

A Note on the Author

Larry Gray grew up in Ohio. After attending the University of Dayton and graduate school at the University of Notre Dame, where he received a Ph.D. in English
literature, he and his wife, Beth, lived in Cannes, France, for a year. Then, having
secured a job as a professor in the English department of Southeastern Louisiana University, they moved to Hammond, Louisiana, where they have been ever since. They have two
children, Ian and Juliet, and six grandchildren with another on the way.

Besides his family, Larry has two loves: writing and theater. Since his earliest days,
he has written fiction, and his stories have appeared in many magazines and journals. His
novel, *Rounding Third and Heading for Home*, is available on Kindle. In theater, he has
worked as an actor, director, and playwright. His plays have been produced in New York,
Chicago, New Orleans, Buffalo, Memphis, and London, among other cities.

When his grandchildren asked him, "Tell us a story," he couldn't say no—and the
result was two volumes of children's stories, *The Land of the Three Elves*, parts I and II,
published by Outskirts Press. *Bayou Coeur and Other Stories* is his first published collection of stories for adults. He is hard at work writing more.

Lightning Source UK Ltd.
Milton Keynes UK
UKHW03f1816300418
321900UK00001B/96/P